THE STORYTELLER

KINGDOMS

THE STORY TELLER

KINGDOMS

A Gallery of Biblical Portraits

Steve Stephens

PROMISE
PRESS
An Imprint of Barbour Publishing

© 2000 by Steve Stephens

ISBN 1-57748-677-3

Cover illustration: Lookout Design Group
　　　　　　　　http://www.lookoutdesign.com

Published by Promise Press, an imprint of Barbour Publishing, Inc., P.O. Box 719, Uhrichsville, Ohio 44683, http://www.barbourbooks.com

Member of the
Evangelical Christian
Publishers Association

Printed in the United States of America.

DEDICATION

To all who are willing to consider. . .
the strength of King-Maker,
the comfort of Hope-Giver, and
the reality of Truth-Holder.

ACKNOWLEDGMENTS

The author gratefully acknowledges those whose lives and support have been integral to retelling these stories of King-Maker, Hope-Giver, and Truth-Holder.

- As always, Tami, who is by my side and in my heart.

- My parents, who provided a home where faith, family, and fun were abundant.

- My brothers and sisters (Becky, Debbie, Dale, James, and Jon), who will always be friends.

- My in-laws, Bill and Sue, who are great parents and wonderful grandparents.

- Uncle Walt, who puts up with us every Labor Day weekend.

- Paul Ingram, who patiently makes my words sparkle, even when deadlines loom.

- Susan Schlabach and all the supportive people at Promise Press, who have stood by this project through thick and thin.

- All those friends, relatives, clients, and acquaintances who have encouraged me to continue this work.

INTRODUCTION

I love these stories.

Some are well-known to those who read the Scriptures. Some are often overlooked in the detail of the story of the people of Palestine. I heard many of them, told in more traditional words, at the knee of my mother and grandmother. Others I did not hear until after I was a graduate student under the tutelage of scholarly men of God.

The stories of *Kingdoms* are fascinating and alive and vital. They teach us much about human nature and relationships and faith. They expose the truth of who we really are. That's both comforting and frightening, because some of the people you will meet in these pages were not very "nice." The best of them had rough edges. Yet there is a relevance to their personalities.

Their stories stretch our minds
and sometimes touch our hearts
and inevitably deepen our souls.

The purpose of this book is to creatively retell, through the voice of the man of a hundred wrinkles, the stories of three "double books" of the Hebrew Scriptures: 1 and 2 Samuel, 1 and 2 Kings, and 1 and 2 Chronicles. Look closely and you will even see a little borrowing from the Poets— Psalms, Proverbs, and Ecclesiastes.

But why retell these old familiar stories?

For one thing, they are no longer familiar. I know that many of you who pick up this book have never heard them before. If that is the case, you are in for a delightful surprise. Romance, treachery, bloody battles, and epic scenes of grandeur. That is the subject matter of the scriptural books that these stories try to convey.

If you remember who David and Solomon are, from the golden days of ancient Israel, you may have more trouble keeping straight the likes of Abijah and Amaziah, Nadab and Omri and Zimri. Even keeping straight those Cinderella's wicked step-sisters—Athaliah and Jezebel—can be a chore.

In these struggles we try to help you by giving names that relate to some aspect of each character's story. But don't feel guilty if it gets a little muddled at times. Simply approach them as people. Relax and let the New Land become your address. Listen to the songs sung by Shepherd. Dream the dreams of Sailor. Marvel at the faithful miracle-workers Listener and Seer. More important, in these thirty-one stories, learn about the one who is King-Maker and Hope-Giver and Truth-Holder. For the one above the sky is always close and will always care.

This is the third book in the story teller series. I hope you have had a chance to enjoy *Beginnings* and *Leaders*. I also encourage you to look for the fourth and final part of the story, *Promises*.

PART 1
THE KING-MAKER

TABLE OF CONTENTS
THE KING-MAKER

PROLOGUE

Days began early for shepherds and could last very late. The work was hard and the sun hot. It was good that so many families of shepherds could live side by side and shear wool and share the care of their sheep. That did mean there were more sheep to eat the limited grass, so the shepherd families had to move frequently to fresh pastureland.

They had taken their tents down and moved them several miles and pitched them once more. After their journey, everyone relaxed around a roaring fire with the contentment that comes in exhaustion. Only the children still had energy left. They played a running game just beyond the circle in the dancing light of the reddish-yellow flames. They shouted and laughed and waved their arms.

The oldest man among them wearily stood up. By the time he had worked out the soreness of joints and muscles, the game had ended. The children joined their families until the circle was complete. Everyone looked at the storyteller with restless anticipation. Some of his stories were exciting and some brought tears and some were frightening. What was most amazing about the stories told by the gray-bearded man was that each was true and was a part of their own history.

The man with a hundred wrinkles moved slowly, meticulously toward the center. His plain wool robe glowed with the brightness of the fire. Then he began to speak:

"The first kings were like us, people who lived by cattle and sheep. They listened to stories of Garden-Maker and Promise-Keeper around fires on cold desert nights. They knew the promise of the rainbow. The one beyond the sky is always near and he always cares.

"But then they were chosen by a King-Maker to govern people instead of sheep. Of course only the one above all makes kings out of shepherds. It is the same one who makes blue planets and gardens and rainbows. It is the one who makes sheep and kingdoms. He it was who made the first three kings.

"They were powerful and weak.

"They were wise and foolish.

"They lived lives of intense good and desperate evil."

The man of a hundred wrinkles stopped speaking for a long moment and peered into the fire.

"The first kings lived our most wonderful dreams and our worst nightmares," he continued in a whisper alive with mysterious foreboding. "So listen not to tales of great kings.

"Listen to the wind.

"Listen to the consuming fire.

"Listen to the power of King-Maker."

WHAT ONE LOOKS FOR
IS OFTEN NOT SO IMPORTANT
AS WHAT ONE FINDS.

CHAPTER 1

THE SECRET PRINCE

Tomorrow."

The low whisper floated on the breeze. The old man stood on a sun-drenched hilltop and looked up. The one known as Speaker showed neither surprise nor fear.

"Tell me about tomorrow," he said, looking beyond wisps of clouds—beyond even the sky. The refreshing message rustled his cloak:

"Tomorrow you shall look into the eyes of the future.

"You shall see a warrior to free my people.

"You shall meet a man to be their king."

"Oh, that I might set down this weight of your people," Speaker sighed. "But how will I know this man? How will I judge his worth?"

"I am Sculptor of People and Maker of Kings," sang the breeze. "Long ago I shaped the Blue Planet and planted a garden and fashioned a man from mud beside the stream. I bore the weight of this people long before I made you the speaker. I will mold a humble heart, who walks at my side through the highlands and shuns the ways of Shining One. The man you meet will be worthy, because I declare him so. I am King-Maker."

The following day, two tired and dirty and bedraggled men trudged the road. For three long days the son and the servant had hiked the central highlands, looking for a herd of donkeys that had been spooked by wild animals and tore into the hills. Nowhere could they be found.

Beneath the sweat and grime of the taller man was the son of a wealthy landowner, owner of the donkeys and many other cattle and sheep and goats.

"They would not come this far," he said. "If we search much longer, we will have no food."

"I agree," said the servant, "but look at the village on yonder hill. That's the city of Speaker. He walks with the one who holds stars in his hands, and he knows many secrets. If we ask him about our donkeys, he will know."

"I should ask the most respected man in our nation to point us toward a few donkeys? No, this is too little to bring to such a great man," said the son. "We lack even a gift to show our gratitude for his attention."

"I will gladly give this silver coin even to stand near this man," said the servant. "Remember that my master, your father, fought beside him many springs ago. I believe we should dare it."

As the two approached the city walls it was late. Young women with large jars drew water from the well as the son approached them. One giggled and another blushed, for they could see a handsome man beneath the layers of sweat and dust.

"Where would we find Speaker?"

"At this hour you will find him climbing that hill," answered one of the women. "Each evening he sacrifices a spotless, newborn lamb to King-Maker with any who care to gather there. If you hurry, you can catch up with him."

The two easily caught up with the crowd who gathered about a bent grandfather. The air was filled with the bleat of a protesting lamb, whose trussed legs were slung across the shoulders of a young boy. As the travelers neared the procession, the old man stopped and turned toward them.

"Forgive our interruption," began the son respectfully. "May we ask your help?"

A smile flickered across the weathered face.

"The donkeys already are found," he said calmly with a penetrating gaze into the tall traveler's deep brown eyes.

"You know about the donkeys?" asked the servant in disbelief.

"Every hoof that makes a track across the Blue Planet stands in the shadow of King-Maker," Speaker answered. His eyes had not left the younger man, who felt self-consciously uncomfortable. Suddenly the man turned back to his path, but he continued his conversation, as if the two newcomers were his only companions. The others, some in rich, fine garb, glanced at them in curiosity.

"These are the elders of our people. Some have traveled many miles today at my summons. I have called them to a feast this night. Look well, everyone, at my tall young friend. He is the reason you have come."

As all eyes turned toward him, the young man stopped in shock. "There must be a mistake. You wait for someone else. I am but a humble herdsman in search of lost donkeys." His voice was tense as he felt a sudden thrill.

"I am an only son.

"Ours is the smallest tribe of the new land.

"And my father is not among the elders."

The old man trudged on. Reaching the crest, he placed the lamb on the stone and lifted his arms toward the sky. With an expert stroke the lamb's life flowed across the stone. A fire of thanksgiving consumed the tiny body, and the shepherds joined the old man and elders in a familiar song of love to King-Maker. As sweet smoke drifted above the Blue Planet, Speaker turned to the people.

"A king has been chosen! When the time is right, the new land shall know his name."

"Not me." the son whispered in unbelief. "He cannot be thinking of me!" Speaker put his arm around the son, and they led the way down the hill in quiet conversation.

"King-Maker makes noble use of a tiny lamb," remarked Speaker.

"He delights in the simple.

"He finds nobility in the lowly."

A crowd waited in the banqueting hall, actually the open courtyard of the house where Speaker lived and judged the people. It was the largest building of the village. The travelers were given water for washing their hands and faces. As the sun lingered on the horizon and torches were lit, Speaker led the son to the head table.

"We can't sit here," protested the young man. "I should not be here at all, and surely not at the table of honor."

"You deserve to be here more than any other person in this room. You have been chosen."

So the perplexed herdsman was seated in the best place and was served first the best piece of roast lamb.

"Who is that man?" wondered the leaders. No one could think what noble family was represented in this handsome, muscled warrior. Speaker answered none of their questions. After the meal the old man and his two guests sat on the flat roof under a million stars. They talked of battles past, and the wonderful acts of King-Maker when he was known by the people as Promise-Keeper and Bondage-Breaker. Finally they nodded into peaceful, dreamless sleep.

As the sun first lit the Mountains of the Dawn, Speaker walked alone with King-Maker. "What shall I do with the young man?"

"Anoint him to be set apart, but tell no one his name. When the time is right I shall reveal him."

As the son and the servant prepared to leave the city, Speaker pulled the future king to the side. "Tell your servant to go on ahead, but you stay here and I shall give you a message from King-Maker."

The son sent the servant on ahead, and Speaker took a jar of the sweetest olive oil. "Come with me," he said. They went to a shaded, secluded place outside the walls. "Kneel," ordered Speaker.

With a hundred questions flooding his mind, the son obeyed and felt the golden oil dribble down his neck, around his ears, and into his dark beard. A kiss brushed both sides of his face.

"Rise, future king. You will save the People of the Promise from their enemies. You will bring power and justice and unity to this nation."

Speaker continued: "I will confirm my words with three signs. First you will meet two men with good news. Then three men will come with food. Last, you will meet a group of men who lift their eyes beyond the sky. When you see them your vision will grow clear and your eyes also will be drawn beyond the sky. From that moment on you will never be the same."

Hours after the son left the city he met two of his father's servants sitting by the side of the road.

"What are you doing so far from home?" he asked the men.

"We are looking for you. The donkeys wandered home, but you did not, so your father sent us to seek you."

"Hurry home," said the son. "Tell my father that I am well and will see him shortly."

The day grew hot and the road dusty. The son rested in the shade of an ancient oak. Three men on their way to sacrifice on the hill with Speaker also stopped. They took off their sandals and soaked their feet in a small spring and shared their goat cheese and bread with the son.

Continuing on his way, he met a group of young men singing and dancing and shouting of King-Maker.

"Why are you so joyful?" asked the son.

"How can we be silent, when King-Maker is always close and he always cares?" said a young man.

"Who told you that?"

"We are students of Speaker," said the young man. "He has taught us many things about the one above all. It has changed our lives. Come, join our dance!"

The son stood apart, but watched and listened to the lyres and tambourines, to the rhythms of clapping hands and stamping feet. He watched as dancers spun into a circle and away again, apart and away, apart and away.

His mind drifted through the past day. King-Maker had always seemed important but distant from daily life. Now, suddenly King-Maker stood at his very center, demanding and calling and pulling him forward into the music and a new reality.

His feet moved of their own will, and memory spun his mind backwards. Again he stood among his father's sheep in the hills north of the City of Palms. He had been alone, yet always he felt a presence.

Now the scene changed. He sat among children listening to an elder tell the ancient stories of one who had revealed himself as Garden-Maker and Promise-Keeper and Bondage-Breaker and Land-Giver and People-Builder. Now he had added a new name—King-Maker. What did it mean to him?

The son remembered stories of the Garden and the Flood and how General had led their escape from the Land of Deltas. He had never listened to the invitation to walk through the morning with the one who holds stars in his hands. It all seemed so confusing.

Yet it was so clear. He had only to look up. Two innocent eyes focused on the sky and a gentle wind welcomed him to a more meaningful existence. A brilliant light surrounded him and his entire body tingled as King-Maker
touched his spirit,
softened his heart,
changed his life.

The words of Speaker echoed through the rhythm of the music: "From that moment on you will never be the same."

The future king lost himself in the memories and stories and music. He would have been surprised to see himself beating a tambourine and weaving through the other dancers, a look of joy glowing in his eyes. Then the group climbed a nearby hill and sacrificed a spotless, newborn lamb to the one who changes lives.

Late that night the son returned home. His father and his cousin greeted him warmly with concern and questions. He patiently told them about the search and the city and the meeting with Speaker. But he demanded that his servant say nothing about the words of Speaker, and he said nothing about his future or the change in his life.

But his relatives could not help but notice that the humble herdsman who had left four days earlier was no more. There was a confidence and a peace and a sense of purpose. Most surprising, early each morning, before the sun lit the Mountains of the Dawn, he arose and walked the highlands with King-Maker.

FOOLS ELBOW FORWARD
ON THE PATH OF EXPEDIENCE;
THE PRUDENT MAKE HARDER CHOICES
TOWARD A MORE EXCELLENT DESTINATION.

CHAPTER 2

THE FIRST KING

The people of the land grew restless. Had not Speaker promised them a king? Was he simply trying to hold his place of authority? He was an old man, soon to go to King-Maker's house beyond the sky, yet the people felt no closer to their desire. They grumbled and complained.

Then messengers were seen running through the land: "Everyone, come to the City of the Tower. Men and women and children—Speaker calls all the people of the New Land. Gather on the field where he led us against the soldiers of the sea many years ago!"

The herdsman and his father and his cousin and many servants joined the ever-growing throng. But none walked as uncertainly as did the herdsman. It had been thrilling to be feasted and anointed and to imagine what being king would be like.

But what if now was the time? He was not ready, . . .not yet!

At the appointed hour the great open field had become a crowded festival grounds. Speaker climbed to a high wooden platform. His aged voice still thundered across the expanse.

"People of the Promise. You asked for a king. Today you shall have one. King-Maker will reveal the leader he has chosen! Prepare the lots."

Elders representing each of the twelve great kindreds stepped forward with the lots.

The honored tribe was selected. From this people a king would come. Incredibly, the smallest tribe was chosen. Elders of that kindred stepped forward to cast lots.

A division was chosen
and a clan

and then a single family.

Finally the lot fell to a single man—one that none of the tribal elders could remember meeting. Or had they? Was he the young man they had celebrated at the banquet at Speaker's home?

The crowd applauded and cheered and waited with excited anticipation. But moments turned into long, drawn-out minutes. No one came forth. People looked about in confusion and curiosity and concern. Only Speaker seemed unworried. He whispered to the elders, who hurried away.

The enthusiasm had become a murmur.

Speaker raised his hands. "Peace, brothers and sisters. It seems our new king is less happy about King-Maker's choice than we are. He is hiding."

Uneasy laughter rippled through the crowd. What sort of king would hide?

The herdsman cowered between two wooden carts on the edge of the meeting grounds, where the oxen were fed. He wrestled with sheer terror.

"I have chosen you," whistled the wind in his ears.

"I am not as close to you as was General, nor am I as wise as Speaker. I am reserved and simple and unschooled," said the son. "I've not led an army or organized a kingdom. I cannot rule a people."

"That is good," said the wind. "As long as you remember your weakness, you will be a great and worthy king. Listen to my words and walk where I lead, then all will be well."

"But the people expect so much."

"They will be patient. You are chosen. It is time to accept your future. Now, stand tall and take the place I have given to you."

The herdsman peeked over the carts. A dozen elders moved his way. He stood straight and stepped forward to meet them. They escorted him through the crowd to the platform where Speaker extended his hands in welcome.

"People of the New Land—behold, First King!"

This is a tall and handsome man, thought many in the crowd. He had a shy humility. Now the cheers echoed twice as loudly, for King-Maker's grand choice fit their best expectations. Shouts rang out:

"Long live First King!"

"May his reign prosper!"

"In greatness will he lead!"

Speaker placed his arm around the king and said, "You have been chosen and anointed and accepted, but you will not be crowned until you are tested in battle."

So First King returned home to build an army. He did not lack, for many wanted to be valiant warriors in the first army of the new kingdom. Where sheep had grazed, a great training encampment was pitched. The king's uncle, who had fought well in the first war against the Sea People, was made commander. Training was immediate, for time was short. War bands from the People of the Plains would soon cross the eastern border. Sea warriors held strongholds across the central highlands and threatened a new invasion from the west. Squeezed between powerful enemies, First King prepared his warriors and listened to King-Maker.

And worried.

After a cycle of the moon, a messenger rushed into camp. "The plains warriors are moving against the east bank," said the exhausted runner.

The king of the Plains People was strong and cruel. He had made a pact with Shining One and now sent his soldiers to burn and kill and maim. They surrounded the City of Safety in the borderland near the Winding River. The city had one week to surrender or face annihilation.

"We are the last free city on the east bank. You are our only hope," they told First King.

"King-Maker gave us the new land. King-Maker will defend it," urged First King with fire in his voice. "The City of Safety will not fall so long as I have strength to lift a blade."

First King ordered preparations for battle. But as he assembled his men he saw that he did not have the force needed to defeat the warriors of the plains.

"We need the united help of all ten tribes," the king said.

"They won't fight," remarked the commander. "They will wait to see if you act as a true king."

"Very well. We shall see how a king acts," resolved First King as he marched into his father's animal pens with a large ax. People watched mystified as he separated two large oxen and cut their throats. Lifting the ax high above his head, he chopped the dead animals into ten large pieces. He gave a bloody piece of sinew and bone and hide to ten teams of messengers.

"Go to your tribes with this gift. Tell them to join me at the City of Safety, or my soldiers will do the same to their oxen."

The deadline for surrender was at hand, but now a great army of rescuers stood by the Winding River, within striking distance of the enemy troops. When the night was darkest, three battalions forded Winding River and approached the enemy camp from three directions. Silently they surrounded the Army of the Plains and moved in for the attack. The guards who kept watch were asleep and had no time to sound the alarm. They were struck down quietly and quickly. Before dawn, First King and the commander lifted their swords. With shouts to King-Maker, the army stampeded through the camp.

What enemy soldiers survived the attack ran for their lives, many without weapons or even clothing.

The battle was won.

The city was saved.

One enemy was defeated.

First King had proven himself, and Speaker set a golden crown on his dark and handsome head.

"King-Maker can cast the noblest forms from the simplest elements," Speaker reminded the people. As the cheer rang, a breeze whispered in the young king's ear: "Now you face your greatest foe—yourself. It is a small thing to humble the heart of a herdsman. But can you conquer the pride and power and privilege of a king? Follow closely, or else fall to Shining One."

Not many cycles of the moon later, Speaker stood before the leaders of the land, his head bent and his shoulders slumped. The people watched with gratitude the man who had led them so faithfully for so many years.

But a tear of disappointment ran down the old man's face.

"At the end of my days I lodge my complaint against you. The one beyond the sky has given you a New Land and supplied every need. You have the king you desired. But already you show a lack of wisdom. You trust in a king, rather than the one who makes kings."

"We can follow both."

"But you cannot. Choose one or the other, or your loyalties will be as divided as your love for King-Maker. Kings turn from truth. If you follow a king before King-Maker, this land will soon grow dark."

As if in illustration, a shadow passed before the sun. Thick gray clouds blew in from the west, swallowing the light.

Thunder shook the hills.

Lightning split the sky.

Rain soaked the people.

Out of the darkness came Speaker's voice: "Fear not, for King-Maker will not leave you." At these words the torrent quieted to a sprinkle, and the sky began to clear.

"Follow his ways. Never forget his power. If you turn your back to him, you and your king will be swept away."

The People of the Sea watched the new king. Their spies reported that a small but sturdy fortress was rising in a forest of pine and cypress. Already the Sea People had been pushed back in skirmishes through the rugged hill country.

First King also had spies, who watched the sea soldiers and their strongholds in the central highlands. Tension grew, and clashes increased in frequency and violence. The king of the Sea People remained confident. He had more warriors and stronger weapons.

"Let the children build their sand fortresses and pretend," he told his generals. "If they become annoying, we will crush them."

Prince, First King's eldest son, was a courageous man of more than twenty summers. He respected Speaker and followed King-Maker better than did his father. Prince learned that a stronghold of the enemy had been left under the guard of a small force. Here was opportunity.

With a thousand men, he surrounded and attacked and destroyed the fortress. The people celebrated, and Prince was a hero. The furious People of the Sea plotted revenge.

Now runners came from the west. "The Sea People have horsemen and chariots and foot soldiers as plentiful as the sands by the sea."

First King sent messengers with rams' horns through the New Land. They blew the battle cry. When warriors heard, they parted from their families and journeyed to the city overlooking the Winding River. Within days an army had gathered.

The forces of the sea cut violently across the central highlands and held a pass connecting the lowlands with the Winding River. When the Army of the Kingdom saw the strength of their enemy, their hearts were fearful. Some hid in caves and cliffs and cisterns. Others crossed the Winding River and fled to the borderlands.

First King calmed and encouraged the troops. "King-Maker is stronger than the greatest enemy. He is our sword and shield and strength."

"Let's offer spotless, newborn lambs to ask King-Maker to give us victory," said the leaders. "No one can stand before the one who is infinite and eternal and all-powerful."

"Only Speaker can offer a sacrifice before battle," said First King. "He will be here soon."

So the soldiers waited, but after seven days Speaker had not arrived. Morale was low and the army was falling apart and the king was impatient.

"Why can't I sacrifice?" murmured the king. "Speaker is not here, and the men won't go into battle without a sacrifice. If we don't do something my army will melt to nothing and the sea soldiers will destroy my kingdom."

"Be patient. Speaker will come," said an advisor.

"The time to wait is past. We must do something." First King turned to his servants and ordered: "Bring me the spotless, newborn lambs."

With his battle sword, the king offered the lambs on the altar. But the smoke was not sweet.

"What have you done?" boomed the voice of Speaker. He had watched the rising smoke as he approached.

"I had no choice," said the king. "You are late."

"So you ignored the way of King-Maker," said Speaker. "You have not kept your word. Therefore, the kingdom will not pass to your children. Power corrupts your heart. If you continue in your pride, you will be replaced by a king with a soft heart."

Speaker turned his back and walked into the hills. First King gathered what was left of his army and returned home. When the warriors of the sea saw no opposition, they sent war parties to plunder.

They burned fields
and destroyed houses
and killed all in their path.

And for more years, the land awaited its salvation.

A SECOND CHANCE IS A TREASURE
THAT SOME NEVER GET,
OTHERS NEVER APPRECIATE,
AND MOST SQUANDER.

CHAPTER 3

THE LAST CHANCE

You have done much to disappoint the one who made you."

The old man did not speak with anger, nor with the fear one might have when bringing a complaint against a powerful king. First King had indeed become powerful.

No, Speaker simply stated what both he and the king knew to be fact. In the presence of Speaker, First King still felt the awe he had known as a young man when he had asked the great follower of King-Maker to help him find his lost donkeys. Unfortunately, in twenty summers as king of the New Land, he had never felt that sense of awe in the presence of King-Maker himself.

Sometimes he only halfheartedly believed in the one beyond the sky — the one who had established his kingdom. First King had become accustomed to believing in the rock-hard realities of political power and military strength. Might that could not be seen did not seem so mighty. On the other hand, there was a strength and an authority owned by Speaker that seemed beyond the realities of envoys and negotiations and advisors.

But then Speaker was of another time, and that time was rapidly becoming a dim memory.

Dim memory or not, the old man who cast a piercing eye on him as he sat in his council chamber was all too real. He inwardly quaked and wished Speaker would simply go away.

"How far we have come, my son, from the day you danced in adoration before the presence of King-Maker? How many summers has it been since you walked the highlands before the dawn of day to seek his face? Why is it that. . .

"you no longer listen to the wind

"or look beyond the sky

"or follow faithfully?"

The king feebly protested with the guilty look of a boy caught stealing from the village fruit trees.

"You know I have asked the people to seek only King-Maker. I have ordered from our borders all the priests of Shining One and all who seek the voices of the dead. Have you ever lacked lambs for sacrifice these twenty summers? I simply do not have the time to be alone with King-Maker as when I herded sheep and donkeys. If you were a king you would understand that. . . ."

He would have gone on like this but for the silencing gesture of the hand of Speaker.

"Yes, you are too busy to bother with King-Maker; that has brought ruin to you and your people. You walk with King-Maker just as far as the path goes in the direction you would travel anyway. Pride is your ruler and will be your destruction and the destruction of your entire family. Still, I have gone to King-Maker to plead for you, and he will give you one final chance to be the king he anointed you to be."

"Another chance?"

"A last chance to behave as the true king of King-Maker, to become once again the humble follower of what is true and right and good."

The king remembered the closeness he had once felt to King-Maker, and he felt a shudder for the implied danger that his throne was in jeopardy.

"Whatever he would have me do, I will do it."

"The people are still in grave danger of turning from King-Maker. The People of the Desert continually entice them to follow Shining One, just as they did when our fathers first prepared to enter the land. You can end this threat and stand for King-Maker before all the world.

"What you must do is severe but necessary," said Speaker. "Journey south and destroy the Desert People. Kill every one of them and all their animals. Regard everything that breathes in that land as cursed. Nothing is to be left. Have no mercy on men or women, children or infants, cattle or sheep or camels. Execute justice on the mortal enemies of King-Maker."

"I will do exactly as the one above the sky has asked," said First King. "When my army is finished, not one person or animal of the Desert People will breathe the fresh air of the Blue Planet."

Speaker turned and walked away. *We shall see,* he thought sadly.

First King gathered a great army of foot soldiers and marched to the southern border of the New Land. The Desert People had one major city, set in a mountainous wilderness that invaders had never penetrated. But First King did not try to take the city directly. Instead he set an ambush in the ravine that led to the capital city. So well did he organize and carry out the attack that the king of the Desert People did not know of the invasion until all was in place. He sent his own raiders out carelessly, into the waiting swords of First King. Thus the army came to be destroyed and the city fell. Survivors fled into the great desert. First King and Prince left their bodies scattered across the dry wilderness as far as the eastern frontier of the Land of the Delta. With swords raised high, they killed all their enemy and all their animals.

Or almost all. In one secret valley the army came upon the Desert King himself. He was hiding with his own flocks of sheep and cattle.

The Desert King fell at the feet of First King:

"You are a great and fearsome warrior, First King," he shouted. "I would delight to be your humble servant and to place all my fine herds into your hand. There are no better animals anywhere. I have silver and gold hidden, with which to ransom my life."

"Why haven't you killed the Desert King?" Prince asked his father that night before the blazing fire. "The one above all told us to leave nothing alive."

"And I have done as he asked, except for sparing the enemy king himself, whose fathers established a trading empire that has thrived for centuries. Think what it would mean to have his connections. Consider what his fine breeding stock will do for our nation. If he is left alive he also promises to reveal the location of a fortune in silver and gold," said First King. "King-Maker wants his people to thrive. He surely wants us to have these things."

Prince looked at his father with concern. "The one who holds stars in his hands needs no silver or gold," he muttered.

"With it we will build the grandest temple the Blue Planet has ever seen. With it, King-Maker will make our dynasty great."

The animals were driven across the river, followed by the army. Along the road, one of the soldiers ran back to First King.

"Master. It is the old one. He is standing in the road ahead, waiting for us."

First King rode a fine stallion, the war horse that had been Desert King's. He urged his mount forward with sudden, foreboding fear. He did not have to ask who this old one was.

When he reached Speaker, the old man looked the picture of an ancient shepherd, for he was standing in the midst of a river of bleating white wool. The great flock was swirling around his legs and on down the road. He was not looking at the sheep being driven around him, though. His eyes were fixed on the fine figure of a king astride a dark charger.

First King slid from his mount and waded through the sheep with a smile that he hoped was bright enough to hide his churning insides. The king wrapped his arms around Speaker.

"May King-Maker bless you!"

But Speaker's body was tense, and he did not return the embrace.

"I have destroyed the Desert People," the king said. He had to shout over the noise around him. "I have done everything King-Maker asked of me."

Speaker looked around. "I am having trouble hearing you with these old ears," Speaker said evenly. "It must be the sound of all this bleating and mooing."

"My soldiers captured them from the Desert People. They spared the best sheep and cattle. I plan to sacrifice each of them to King-Maker. But we totally destroyed the rest."

"I did not come to hear your excuses," said Speaker. "I came to tell you what King-Maker said to me last night. Do you wish to know?"

"Please, tell me."

"Here are the words of King-Maker: 'You were a humble herdsman with a soft heart. You promised you would not follow Shining One, as other kings of other kingdoms. Yet that is what you became: a selfish liar who has joined in alliance with the very king I sent you to destroy.'"

"I have not! I destroyed the Desert People, just as he asked!"

"Be still! Do you challenge the judgment of the one who looks into every heart? He has stood by you these twenty summers, even when you turned from him. He gave you a final opportunity to prove you would follow. Has he done so little for you, that you refused to do as he asked?"

A sob of the lawbreaker before the judge caught in the throat of First King. "I completely destroyed the Desert People except for those who ran to the Land of the Delta. . .and their king. My soldiers killed their animals . . .except for these. And I will sacrifice every head."

Speaker looked at him with love, thinking of the man he had been, the king he might have been, had he only followed King-Maker.

"My friend. It is not enough to go through the motions now that you have been caught in your deception. It is better to follow his ways than to give the sweetest sacrifice. Now hear the judgment of King-Maker. Because you reject his command, he rejects your crown."

First King fell to the ground.

"Please tell him that I admit it. I have failed. But it was the fault of the people. They wanted to bring back the Desert King and the best sheep and the strongest cattle. I tried to please them, instead of the one above all. Please come and sacrifice a spotless, newborn lamb for me, so the one beyond the sky might give me one more chance."

Speaker turned his back in disgust. He began to walk away. First King reached out to stop him and grabbed the hem of his robe. With a rip, a piece of fabric tore away.

"Please stop," wept the king. "Without my kingdom I am nothing."

Speaker turned to face the king.

"Without King-Maker you are nothing. As this fabric ripped away, so your kingdom will be ripped from you and your sons. It will be given to another. I will ask King-Maker to grant you something you lost twenty summers ago."

"What was that?" sobbed the king.

"A humble heart."

It was a request that would not be granted. For long months Speaker mourned the fall of the humble herdsman and never again spoke to the king. First King became increasingly selfish and bitter and lonely. The soft heart that had walked the highlands with King-Maker turned to stone.

His mind, and the land around him, grew dark with treachery.

CHAPTER 4

THE SHEPHERD BOY

I hate him!" he yelled with red face and white knuckles. A wine goblet of fine silver clattered off the wall across the room. As they had been instructed by Prince, the servants remained out of sight, waiting until the fit of rage subsided. The drunken fits of First King were increasing in frequency; not one was safe in his presence.

"I hate him! I hate him! I hate him!" he screamed until his voice was hoarse. All night long he paced—muttering and cursing, throwing things and ripping his clothes, drinking and threatening anyone who dared reason with him.

Prince sent a warning to Speaker: "Since you confronted my father with his failure, he blames you for all that goes wrong. He knows he has lost the crown, but he refuses to submit to the will of King-Maker. He says he will kill anyone who tries to take it from him. I fear for your safety."

Life was slipping out of control—anger. . .confusion. . .fits of rage. . . depression. . .hopelessness. . .self-loathing. . . The cycle began anew as the sun dipped below the western horizon. The nights were endless.

Those closest to First King feared that if the people knew his state of mind they would rise up to demand a new king. All hoped he would get better; instead, each day his hold on reality seemed more slippery.

As Speaker slept, a wind swept down from the hills through his open window. He was gently shaken to consciousness.

"Rise up," the voice said. "I send you to the City of Hope. Fill your horn with olive oil to anoint a new king for my people."

Now he was fully awake.

"To get to the City of Hope, I must pass First King's fortress. If he sees me he may suspect my purpose. Whether he does or not, he will kill me by his own hand."

"Take a sacrifice to the elders of the city. Ask for the grandson of Outsider. He has eight sons, and I have chosen one of them."

Speaker came safely to the City of Hope. The elders greeted him with joy and they gathered together the people to make a sacrifice to King-Maker. As the smoke curled skyward, Speaker drew aside with the grandson of Outsider.

"I require a bed this night," he said simply.

"Master, I will be greatly honored if you would stay in my home. There are several of us, but we do not lack for room."

Like many families who were blessed with land and flocks and many children, the grandson and great-grandchildren and great-great-grandchildren of Outsider had built onto their mud-brick home to accommodate each marriage and infant. It had become a mazelike complex of rooms, built according to no particular plan, surrounding a large open courtyard garden. There the shouts and laughter and tears of young brothers and sisters and cousins filled the air each day. The heat from a large brick oven near the entrance to the courtyard was situated as far as possible from the largest room, where all the families gathered to eat, and the women did their work. The great room was as open as possible and situated so as to catch the morning and evening breezes. The whole complex seemed almost a tiny self-sufficient community, where the word of the father and mother had the force of law and the goal of keeping some semblance of order.

"The blessing of King-Maker on this house," Speaker said as he entered the courtyard. "And you are a family most greatly honored by King-Maker, who has sent me on a mission of great joy to you and your sons."

The overwhelmed head of the household lowered his face in awe at these words. Then he quickly assembled his wife and children and grandchildren.

When Speaker met the eldest son, a muscular man with a wise demeanor beyond his thirty summers, he immediately reached for his horn of perfumed oil.

"Stop! What are you doing?" asked the voice of King-Maker.

"I see that you have indeed chosen a great and impressive man to be king. I will anoint him in your name."

"This is not who I have chosen," said the wind. "There is more to a man than being strongest or tallest or most handsome. Those qualities First King had in abundance. People look at outward appearances, but I look at the heart."

So Speaker looked to the second son. He also looked like a fine prospect to lead a nation and an army into battle.

"No," said the wind.

It was the same with the thirdborn and the fourth and the fifth and the sixth and seventh. Each time the whisper in Speaker's ear was a decisive "No."

"Are these all of your sons?" asked Speaker. "I thought you had one more."

"My youngest is some distance away, up in the hills tending the flocks."

"Then send someone to bring him to me, for he is the one I have come to see," said Speaker, "I will not eat nor rest until he stands before me."

The mystified father quickly sent his fastest servants to take his son's place with the sheep and send him back. The actions of the great old man seemed more unfathomable by the moment.

Night was settling on the courtyard and the torches had been lit when a young, wiry boy of fourteen summers sprinted through the gate, panting, his light complexion flushed.

"Behold the next king of the New Land," whispered the wind.

Speaker looked at the small but solidly built lad. He was handsome with deep, sparkling eyes that flickered with good humor. There was a mysterious look about him that Speaker identified at once. Here was one who already wandered the hills with King-Maker.

Speaker put a hand on the shoulder of the boy and felt a last pang of grief. He recalled the day he had last poured his oil over the brow of a prince.

"Kneel before King-Maker," said Speaker. "He who built the Blue Planet and holds the stars in his hands has set his heart upon you. You are ordained to be the next king of the New Land. Walk close to King-Maker and be broken to his will."

A single gasp came from all those gathered in the shadows of the courtyard, under the first stars of the night. The enormity of Speaker's words was inescapable. Only the lad kept his composure as he knelt and felt the oil flow over his face and neck and back, staining the rough wool shirt that covered his body. His eyes sparkled in the glow of the torchlight, while the aroma of the rich perfume was carried on the night breeze to every corner of the house and out into the countryside. Some said later that First King woke that night from a fevered sleep and smelled the fragrance of the oil of anointing. His scream shook the fortress.

The New Land had its next king, but for a time that wondrous news would be the carefully guarded secret of a single family. First King held the crown, but it was slipping away from his grasp toward the head of the boy who tended sheep by the City of Hope.

The best grassy meadows of the highlands could be uncomfortably hot and dry during the day and bitterly cold at night. The life of a shepherd there was hard and uncertain.

Yet the young shepherd was not anxious to trade his lot even for the kingdom he now knew he would one day possess. He loved the rugged beauty as a treasure King-Maker had molded just for him. Sometimes after rain the drab landscape was painted by brightly colored wildflowers. Shepherd could not really imagine what his royal chambers would one day be like. But he was sure they could never be half so beautiful as that hillside, with the sheep cropping the grass contentedly and an ancient olive tree to provide shade.

Sitting in the sparse shade of that ancient monarch, it was difficult to understand what the actions of Speaker meant. He would not worry about it now. All he wanted was the presence of King-Maker and a stringed harp by which to sing to the desert wind and the great band of stars that spread across the night. So he tuned the strings of his lyre until each produced the perfect sound. Then he sang the songs of his heart. The sheep in the peaceful meadow added plaintive voices to the gentle melody.

As the seasons passed, the music grew. Shepherd had a poet's soul and a master's touch on the strings. He could soothe the most skittish flock when wind howled or lightning flashed over the Mountains of the Dawn.

His sweet voice and skilled fingers and sharp wit made him a much-sought guest at weddings and feasts. All who heard him marveled at the clarity and simplicity and emotion of his songs. The music lifted their hearts closer to King-Maker.

As First King's mood swings fluctuated wildly between despair and fury, the men of healing were desperate. It was a servant who suggested that music might be a balm. The prince sought out the finest musicians to ease his father's torments. These musicians alone gave him some peace.

Inevitably news came of a master musician who herded sheep near the City of Hope. So it was that Shepherd first saw the royal courts, feeling a new awe and thrill in remembering the anointing oil of Speaker. On the night he arrived the king was in one of his worst fits.

Furniture was broken.

Pottery was shattered.

Screams and cries and curses echoed.

Shepherd entered the room with his fingers on his lyre and his eyes on the one above the sky. He played his songs softly and confidently as he walked toward the king. His song filled the air and the violence calmed and the wails quieted. Slowly the music took First King back to his own childhood, days of promise when he walked with King-Maker. His tension eased and his terrors subsided. The melody carried him away to peaceful sleep.

"Where do such words and melodies come from?" asked Prince in amazement.

"I simply open my heart and play for the one who holds the stars in his hands. The more I play the closer I get to him."

The shepherd was one of the musicians asked to play often for the king and his guests. More than once a runner begged him to stay at the fortress for a few days, because the king could not be comforted. He patiently tuned each string and skillfully played his music, with every song dedicated to King-Maker. His heart's desire was that the world never forget that the one above all was:

our fortress and our hope,

our calm and our comfort,

our rest and rock and refuge.

The music had an amazing healing effect, and everyone at the court spoke with respect of the shepherd. Even the king liked him, and Prince soon became his closest friend.

During the next several years, whenever the king called, the shepherd came. As time passed the boy grew tall and muscular and fearless. The look of childhood was gone, but he still lacked the years and experience to become what Speaker had anointed him to be.

A TRUE FRIEND
ACCEPTS AND UNDERSTANDS AND DEFENDS
AND GOES A STEP BEYOND
THE EXPECTED.

CHAPTER 5

THE FRIENDSHIP

The warriors of the Sea People crossed the border into the New Land half a day's journey west of the City of Hope. First King moved his troops to block the invasion. The Army of the Kingdom occupied one hill, the Army of the Sea the opposite hill. Both armies wanted to destroy the other, but neither had the upper hand.

Early one morning a sea soldier walked boldly into the valley between the armies. The People of the Kingdom quaked at the sight of him. He was huge, as tall as two men. He glowed and flashed as the morning sun shone off his polished bronze armor. Slung across his back was a huge sword. In his right hand was a spear the size of a sapling. Its iron point had been forged by craftsmen and honed to a glistening point. His voice reverberated along the battle lines.

"I am a killer and a crusher and a destroyer of life! I am Giant, champion of the Sea People. Choose one to face me on the field of combat. Defeat me, and the Sea People will be your servants. If I carry your champion's head from the field, you will serve us forever!"

Soldiers of First King watched Giant in disbelief. They waited for their king, but he lay hidden in his tent—confused and discouraged and fearful. So none stepped from the line to be his champion.

Thus began a morning ritual that brought the kingdom people to despair. Giant marched into the valley, issued his challenge, and taunted his enemies for their cowardice. For forty mornings he stood alone in the valley.

Then a youth arrived in time to hear the bellows and taunts. Shepherd had come to bring his brothers fruits and vegetables. More important, he was to bring back news of the war to a worried father at the City of Hope.

"I grow tired of waiting for you dogs. Send me your god if you are too fearful to come yourselves. Watch as I grind him into dust and drink his blood. Then I will be your god!"

Shepherd listened in rage to the tirade. He waited to see who would teach this large fool not to laugh at the one who holds stars in his hands.

"Why doesn't someone fight him?" the visitor asked his oldest brother. "How can you allow a follower of Shining One to defy the one who is infinite and eternal and all-powerful?"

"You spend your days in peaceful meadows, watching sheep and playing music. What do you know of battle?"

"I don't need to know anything of war to know that man cries against the honor of King-Maker. If the soldiers will not remove this disgrace from the New Land, perhaps you should step aside for the shepherds," the boy said petulantly.

"Take your arrogance and go," shouted the brother, who stalked away with a frustrated curse. So Shepherd took his complaint to the tent of the king.

"What is my court musician doing on the battle lines?" asked the king with a smile.

"Why are you allowing this enemy to cry against King-Maker? Please send me to meet this Giant in combat."

First King was used to being impressed with his young musician. "You are a brave young man, but how could you stand against one who strikes fear in the hearts of seasoned soldiers?"

"I would not go alone. In the highlands, large and ferocious beasts prey on the sheep. I faced them with King-Maker, and he saved me and my sheep from harm. If the one beyond the sky can deliver me from a lion and a bear, what is a defiant giant?"

"You are a brave boy, but I will not send you to your death," said the king.

But his commanders took the request seriously and spoke to the king in private.

"If we do not answer the challenge and break this siege, we will lose the will to fight. Send this boy out. What an insult it will be to the Sea People that we do not even send a soldier to meet their champion. The boy's courage will stir and shame our warriors."

"But he will die."

"Many die in battle. His death could save your kingdom. It is our best hope."

So it was that the army was readied for battle the next morning. They knew a champion would step forward, and they were to charge the field, whatever occurred.

"Kingdom People," Giant rumbled, "we are past impatience! How long must I wait to test your puny god?"

"Wait no longer!" came a cry. "Prepare to fight."

But none stepped from the line.

"Show yourself!" Giant thundered.

"I have," returned the voice. The warrior swung around, seeking the source. Then he noticed the stream that flowed nearby, a young man lounging against a tree on its bank. He wore neither armor nor sword. Slowly he rose and began crossing the grassy field that had been trampled only by Giant. From his right hand hung the familiar leather thong of a sling.

The sling was a common combat weapon. Slingers stood at the front of a battle line to face an enemy charge. They would loose a volley of stones with deadly accuracy. But then they fell back. No soldier carried a sling into personal combat.

"What is this?" rumbled the heavily armored warrior. He turned toward his own army in rage. "Look! They send a child to ridicule me!" He slashed his sword through the air with fury that stole the breath of all who watched—all except Shepherd.

"Throw down your sword," he taunted. "It is worthless against King-Maker!"

Giant sheathed his sword.

"I need no sword, little one, until I cut your body into pieces for the birds." He tossed aside his great shield and lowered the point of his spear. He began to lope across the field.

The shepherd stopped to fit a stone into place. He began the wide sweeping swing of the slinger. The onrushing warrior was covered with armor, but he was quite careless about protecting himself. His only thought was to exact revenge on the boy and the Kingdom People.

"You come against me with sword and spear," the shepherd shouted, "but know that I strike you in the name of King-Maker."

Faster than eye could follow, the hand whipped forward. The stone left its leather pocket with immense force. It struck in front of the flap that protected the warrior's ear.

A dull thud echoed, and the great warrior lurched and was carried by momentum face-first into the grass. He came to rest not many steps from his opponent. In a moment the shepherd was at the side of Giant, pulling the great sword from its sheath and swinging it with all of his strength. The blade imbedded itself in the ground.

There was no sound from either army, so great was the shock, until the boy lifted a bloody head for all to see. The commanders of the Kingdom Army first recovered. They yelled the battle cry and began running down the hill. Now the Army of the Kingdom took up the cry. In another moment the Sea People recovered their wits and fled. Many of them fell that day, and much plunder was taken. Crowds lined the road as word spread.

Men cheered Shepherd.

Women sang and danced.

Children waved in wide-eyed adoration.

Suddenly everybody knew and loved this simple shepherd who walked with the one who holds stars in his hands—all except First King.

"Today he stole the hearts of my people; tomorrow he will steal my kingdom," ranted the jealous king.

"Why does your father look so angry when I play for him?" Shepherd asked.

"You have shown yourself more courageous than he," said Prince.

"I am no threat to your father. As long as he wears the crown, I am his servant."

"But he believes that King-Maker has chosen you to take his place. And I have come to believe it as well. I know that the kingdom has been taken from my family," said Prince sadly. "I will never wear the crown."

Prince took off his royal cloak and laid it on the shoulders of the younger man, over the shepherd's garb.

"I would rather see you wear that crown than any other man I've known. You will serve the people well in the name of King-Maker."

"I cannot accept this," said Shepherd.

"It is token of my pledge to you, the true king. I will be your loyal friend and your devoted subject as long as King-Maker gives me breath."

"I have never known such a friend," said Shepherd.

"I only ask one favor. I fear I will fall to the curse King-Maker set upon my father. I may not live to see you crowned. If not, I would ask your mercy upon my children."

The young shepherd and the older prince locked arms with a bond shared among those who risk everything to walk with King-Maker.

Darker feelings waged battle within the heart of First King when he saw Shepherd—

admiration and hatred,

appreciation and fear,

affection and jealousy.

Shepherd was not allowed to return to his father's sheep in the highlands. He was commanded to play his lyre for the king more often, both for the music and to keep Shepherd where he could be watched. When First King looked upon Shepherd, his spirit trembled and his body shook. No longer did the music soothe his fevers. In one night rage the king hurled a spear at Shepherd, who fled the palace. Within a few days the king was begging him to return.

"I do not want to harm you. I will show my trust by giving you command of a force in my army. We must drive the Sea People back farther. Lead this campaign and I will give my eldest daughter to be your wife."

Shepherd knew this campaign deep in the country of the enemy was dangerous. An inexperienced commander could lose face and life. But he left that to King-Maker and returned after a spectacular victory.

First King was enraged. The king refused to give his daughter to Shepherd, giving her instead to another man with a grand wedding feast. One person was overjoyed at this broken promise. First King's younger daughter had fallen in love with Shepherd and continually found excuses to be with him. They met in the marketplace and walked through the fields by the fortress and sat on the roof to watch the stars make the night spectacular.

"I want only to be with Shepherd," she confided to Prince. "Will you ask Father to give me in marriage to him?"

"He will be angry," said Prince.

But instead the king seemed pleased.

"What is Shepherd willing to give for her hand?" First King asked.

"He loves her deeply, but he has nothing to pay for a bride," Prince said.

"Perhaps there are other ways to pay the price of a princess," answered the king thoughtfully.

The next day word reached Shepherd. First King would give his younger daughter's hand—in exchange for the deaths of one hundred soldiers of the sea. Shepherd immediately disappeared. A few weeks later he was at the king's threshold.

He had not killed one hundred men.

He had killed two hundred.

First King was genuinely frightened by the hardened warrior before him. The king called for his daughter and put her hand in the hand of Shepherd. But more than ever he hated this unstoppable man. Watching the royal wedding he muttered, "You are my son-in-law and my enemy. You will never have my crown."

First King held a secret meeting of his top officers. "I want the death of Shepherd. Whoever brings me his body will be a rich man."

Prince heard and went to Shepherd.

"Leave the city. Hide until his heart changes," he warned.

The next morning Prince confronted his father: "Why are you intent on killing Shepherd? What has he done to wrong you?"

The king was silent.

"Everything Shepherd has done," continued Prince, "has benefited you or the kingdom. He is innocent."

The father listened to his son and his heart was moved. "You are right."

Prince went to the forest and told his friend the good news.

"Father promises on his honor that he will let no harm come to you. He is sorry for his mistrust." For a time there was peace with his father-in-law. But one night that changed forever.

"Come now," gasped the messenger, who had run to Shepherd's dwelling. "It is the king. Come quickly with your lyre before he becomes dangerous."

As Shepherd played, the king first seemed to relax. Then Shepherd sang a song of love to the one above all. Suddenly First King jumped to his feet and grabbed his spear. With a mighty cry he threw the spear with all his strength. Only fast movement saved the life of Shepherd.

He fled north to Speaker and then back to the forests near the fortress. He sent word to Prince, who was leading a force against the soldiers of the sea on the western frontier: "Your father is trying to kill me."

It can't be, thought Prince when he read the message. *On his honor he promised not to allow harm to befall Shepherd.*

"If he was out to kill you, I would know," Prince protested to Shepherd when they met. "But give me time. I will soon know his heart."

This time when Prince approached his father there was no warmth in his eyes. He turned on his son in wrath.

"Disrespectful traitor! I know how you and Shepherd plot behind my back. You conspire with this man who is a threat to your own kingdom! He must die. I want to see blood drain from his body."

Prince secretly left the palace. He had lost a father, but he would not lose his friend.

"May King-Maker guide your steps," said Prince. "You will always be my friend."

Prince returned to the fortress, and Shepherd fled to the hills.

CHAPTER 6
THE FUGITIVE

The cave of refuge was one of many hidden in the rocky hills of the western borderlands, a short journey from the City of Hope. In these caves lived tiny, large-eared mice and red foxes and night owls. Here the deadly carpet vipers slithered, and sleek desert leopards stalked. Shepherd was now a hunted outlaw whose only home was a cave. In desperation he poured out his heart to the one beyond the sky.

"Save me from the ruthless king.

"Rescue me from ravenous assassins.

"Hide me in the shadows of your wings."

A refreshing breeze caressed his brow. "I am with you," said the wind.

As word spread that the hero who had felled Giant was in hiding, men began to arrive at the gates of the City of Hope. Friends of Shepherd guided them to his wilderness cave. Many were distressed and discontented by the actions of First King. Others believed Shepherd would bring the nation to King-Maker. Still others were fugitives themselves or soldiers of fortune who looked for a winner. Dispossessed families found him, so that he was the head of a small community. Tears of joy welled in his eyes as he saw King-Maker answer his cry.

To all he shouted, "Let us follow King-Maker and see where he leads."

Men pointed their swords toward the sky and echoed the words.

Among those who gathered were spies who sent word to the king. Soon a force was nearing the caves. In the dark of night all the hunted slipped past the hunters. For a time they lived the nomadic life of the outlaw. Death was always close. A place was found in the hills south of the Valley of Apples, where the ancestors Merchant and Princess had made a life in the New Land. Shepherd now counted six hundred warriors. He covenanted with them that First King would not die at their hands. Most thought this strange, for First King was relentless in seeking their deaths. Despite his trust in King-Maker, Shepherd sang a song of fear and faithfulness.

"Show me your power.

"Save me from my foes.

"Deliver me from death."

Again he felt the breeze. "I am with you," said the wind.

"But the enemy who seeks my blood is so strong."

"He is not a danger to one who follows me. I am your shield and refuge. I am more than all the forces of Shining One."

"Yes," whispered Shepherd. As he stood lost in thought, a scout ran to him, "We must move quickly," the young man panted. "The king has learned of this place. His soldiers are on the other side of the mountain."

Shepherd looked at his man in disbelief that the danger was so close. "How many stand with him?"

"The countryside is filled with them. He has prepared to fight against us more valiantly than against an army of the Sea People."

"Then there is no place to go," said Shepherd quietly. "He is a cunning commander and surely his men will cut off every retreat."

"Is there nothing we can do?" asked the young warrior.

"Fear not. We will wait on King-Maker to save us from our enemies. Impossibilities do not limit one who is infinite and eternal and all-powerful."

On the other side of the mountain, First King's sentries watched a messenger approach from the direction of the fortress.

"Soldiers of the sea know that the royal city is unguarded. A large force has crossed the western border to take the fortress."

"No!" yelled First King in frustration. "We are too close to pull back now. We must end this traitorous threat."

"It seems you have a choice," said an officer who faced the king intently. "You can take Shepherd or save the royal city. You cannot do both. If the fortress falls, Shepherd's death will be meaningless."

The next morning incredulous scouts gathered before Shepherd.

"They are gone! It is as if the army of First King was never there at all."

"Then bring my lyre and let us gather to thank King-Maker," said Shepherd.

He sat on an outcropping of rock, facing thankful soldiers and their women and children. As he tuned each string, a rare rain dampened the dust. Rays of sunshine sparkled through the sprinkles. An arch of color stretched across the sky.

Shepherd sang, lifting his eyes and lifting his heart and lifting the name of King-Maker. His people could now come out of their hiding places, for King-Maker was their refuge. They stood in the shadow of his wings.

"Surrounded by a thousand lions,

"I need never fear or faint,

"For he is always close and will always care."

The Sea People had been chased from the land. But First King did not join the celebration. He turned his anger on King-Maker. "You are no Promise-Keeper! You chose me to be king, and now you stand by Shepherd, my enemy. I demand that you honor me, your chosen one!"

All was silent.

There was no breeze nor voice.

Speaker did not appear.

Speaker would never come again. The ancient warrior who had anointed First King and been his conscience no longer walked the Blue Planet.

The king felt no sorrow. But he regretted that he could not destroy Speaker for turning against him. So he raged all the more against Shepherd. First King sent for his daughter, Shepherd's bride.

"Beloved daughter, I feel pain that I gave you in marriage to a traitor unworthy of the hand of a princess."

"Father, only you call my husband a traitor."

"Silence! What is the power of this outlaw over my children? Daughter, I declare that you are no longer the wife of my enemy. I have found one who will teach you loyalty. This day you will go to his house and bed. Or you will go to your grave."

Her bitter tears were interrupted by a servant.

"Master, the new camp of Shepherd has been found in the wilderness near the shores of the Salty Sea."

His finest warriors searched the area where the fugitive army had been seen. It was as if the earth had swallowed them all. One hot afternoon during the fruitless search, First King saw a large limestone cave. He posted his guards by its entrance and slept in the dark coolness.

Had First King known more about the region's caves, he might have suspected that this one reached far under the hills, with multiple openings, immense enough to hold a small army.

In fact it did.

As First King slept, Shepherd's commanders faced their leader.

"End it, now! Your vow to protect First King will kill us all. His soldiers will leave us once he is dead. They may even proclaim you the king."

"I will not harm the man King-Maker crowned. But perhaps King-Maker has given us another way to end this madness."

First King awoke from his cool rest. He and two bodyguards had gone a short distance from the cave when he stopped short.

A sound.

A familiar song.

A melody to make the heart melt.

First King turned to see a lone musician perched on a rock, high above the entrance to the cave.

"My king! May you reign long in the footsteps of King-Maker!"

Shepherd set down his lyre and bowed his head before the king. First King stood silent and uncertain and in mortal danger.

"You search for me as if I would harm you," chided Shepherd.

The fugitive lifted a piece of fabric, the hem of a tunic. The king's hand darted to his own clothing. His heart nearly stopped. The bottom of his royal tunic had been sliced away.

"Look! I was in the cave with a sword in my hand while you took your rest. I could have taken your life, but you were as safe as in your bedchamber. Am I truly your dangerous enemy?"

"Oh, my son," cried First King. "How I have wronged you in my hatred, yet you show mercy. I see why the one above all has chosen you to be king. Go in peace. Return with me to the fortress city and I will declare your innocence."

First King gathered his men and returned to the royal city. Shepherd did not go with him. He knew he would not have lived to walk through the gates, whatever the king's promises. But summers passed, and First King no longer pursued Shepherd. Neither was Shepherd pardoned.

But now that there was peace, King-Maker blessed the villages and lands for miles around the Valley of Apples. No longer did marauding Desert bands or Sea raiding parties sweep down to burn the fields and steal the fruit. Robbers did not come out of the caves to attack travelers. Shepherd protected the people and his soldiers planted their own crops and more of their families came to settle.

Then a drought made food scarce. Shepherd sought help to feed his people from the farmers and herdsmen. Most gave what they could to the men who had brought peace and safety and prosperity to their lives.

One man begrudged their request, the region's wealthiest man in land and goats and sheep. He would have been far poorer without their protection, but he was hard-hearted and selfish and mean of spirit.

It was the season to shear sheep when ten young men came to the home of the wealthy herdsman.

"We come to seek your generosity in return for the protection we have given you," said the ten. "In a few days you will celebrate the end of shearing with a feast. May we come to your celebration, or have what is left?"

"Bandits! If you come to my feast uninvited, be prepared to die. Shepherd will get nothing of mine except the edge of my sword."

Such ingratitude was more than Shepherd could bear.

"Take up your swords. This man will answer for his words."

They were nearing the foolish man's land when a scout reported: "Several people come this way. They have oxcarts and drive animals before them."

In a short while a flock of sheep and goats, cows and calves and a fine bull stopped on the road. A beautiful woman in rich clothing astride a donkey leaned over to speak softly to her steward.

"I see no one. Are you sure they are here?"

"Hundreds of eyes are on us, mistress. Arrows rest on many bowstrings."

"Then unload everything in the open area by those trees."

The hidden force looked on in wonderment as servants fitted large boards onto oxcarts to make tables. Meats and breads and vegetables were spread. Abundant earthenware jars of wine waited.

Up among the rocks a man with a large sword slung across his back appeared and made his way to the woman.

"You have picked a strange place to set out a feast," he said. "I and a few fellow travelers have eaten little this day. We would join you if there is more here than you require."

The woman appraised the dark, well-spoken warrior with his well-kept beard.

"This food is not mine. You must ask the one called Shepherd, for it is his table, and all these animals are being taken as a gift to him."

"Who has brought such gifts to this fortunate man?"

The woman's smile was winning and warm. "I am called Joy, for it is said that I brighten all I meet. But my heart is not joyful, for I am married to a foolish man. He has said unforgivable things to the servants of Shepherd, though we should give thanks to King-Maker that Shepherd and his warriors are near. When I find Shepherd I will bow before him and ask his forgiveness."

"Your husband acted foolishly, but he has a wife of rare courage and wisdom and beauty. You have brought joy to my heart and saved me from shedding blood. I am Shepherd, and I have pledged the death of your husband and any who raise a sword alongside him."

"Then before I beg for our lives, call your men from their hiding places so that we may enjoy this food."

Later, as the men looked on, she bowed low before Shepherd.

"Rise, gracious woman. Your spirit has defeated us all. Go home in peace, and may your husband be molded by your example."

Some mornings later, scouts brought news to Shepherd of the surrounding villages.

"I have heard something of the foolish herdsman and his kindhearted wife," said one.

"That magnificent woman!" Shepherd said with a smile. "What a princess she would make if only she was not married to such a man."

"She is now his widow. When Joy told her husband how close he had come to death, he did not respond well. He was angry and unforgiving and resentful.

"His eyes blazed with hatred.

"His fist promised violence.

"His voice threatened harm.

"Then suddenly he froze. He clutched his head and turned his eyes downward and fell at her feet, unable to move. He did not live long. His last words were curses against his wife and against you and against King-Maker."

"King-Maker has brought justice," said Shepherd somberly.

"King-Maker has also brought blessing to my life. This time I will bow at this fair woman's feet and offer to her my heart."

He set off at once, his face brightened by the woman who brought joy.

CHAPTER 7

THE WOMAN OF DARKNESS

The time has come for the New Land to fall," said the king of the Sea People to his council. "The People of the Promise will lie broken. Their king's head will bleach in the sun outside the temple of Shining One."

So the king called the five great cities of the Sea People to war. Thousands of warriors were trained in the arts of death.

Broken swords were reforged and sharpened.

Hides and iron embossments covered shields.

Wheelwrights shaped chariot spokes and rims.

The People of the Sea had grown strong once more. First King had turned back each incursion. But there were stories about his mind. Why else would he try to kill Shepherd, the champion of the People of Promise? It was mystifying, but it showed weakness. The People of the Sea would take advantage of First King's foolishness.

When all was ready, the soldiers of the sea moved north to the Western River and followed it upstream toward the dawn. They traveled through the Valley of Harvests, a fertile landscape with few rocks to break chariot wheels.

The plan was simple: They would cross the Valley of Harvests to the Winding River, thus cutting the New Land in two. The northern and southern tribes were very different from each another. They could not be brought together easily.

The plan was simple and wise.

First King did not pay attention to the vague reports that his enemy was preparing an army. When the invasion came, the small outposts were overrun before they could sound the alarm. By the time First King was aware of the threat, the invaders were halfway across the land. With the standing army available to him, First King raced two days north to the highlands overlooking the Valley of Harvests.

When he looked into the Valley, he understood the scope of the Sea People's action. Their campfires could be seen miles away. By day a vast network of enemy encampments and fortifications was visible. Never had the People of the Promise faced an enemy so numerous and entrenched and well-equipped. Never had First King been so frightened. He could not eat and he could not sleep and he could not lead.

He listened to the wind, but heard no voice.

He looked beyond the sky, but found no presence.

He made panic-stricken vows to King-Maker.

But regardless of his actions, there was no response. "If King-Maker has turned his back, I must go elsewhere," the king reasoned.

"To turn anywhere else is to deny the authority of King-Maker," stated one officer with a pounding fist. "Better to accept the Sea People as our masters than to give our nation to Shining One."

Some agreed. Others were quite ready to turn to Shining One, if they thought he would give them victory.

"We will make our final plan at first light," said the king. He walked absentmindedly away from the commanders, who looked at one another with concern. Decisions were needed now.

But the king was listening to another voice, that of an old man who sat beside his tent. He was one of First King's wisest counselors, or at least it seemed so.

"There are other forces, powers far stronger than your enemy," the old man said.

The grandfather extended his hand to comfort.

"The time has come to look beyond King-Maker. We must consider using different ways to defeat that great army. What we need is a witch."

"A witch, yes," murmured the king. "Find me a witch who can seek guidance from those who have left the Blue Planet."

"But you killed them all," said his old man sadly. "When you became king, you ordered every witch and wizard and caller of the dead removed from the New Land. But I have heard rumors that a few still live in hidden places, practicing the ancient ways. Shall I see what I can learn?"

Within an hour the old man was back.

"Master, I have news. Not a few hours' journey from this spot, a woman lives quietly who serves all who come to her with wise foresight. She is said to have great powers. Let us keep this secret. By dark of night let us ride deep into the hills."

The old man smiled a conspiratorial grin.

A few hours later, a haggard old widow welcomed the strangers. She had dark, piercing eyes and an oddly mystical look. Long gray hair reflected the dim lamplight. Her house smelled strongly of herbs and the dust of ancient parchment. Somehow it all produced an eerie feeling that danger was near.

Before her stood a wizened old man and three tall, strong men who dressed in simple shepherd garb. The old one she knew as a master in the secret ways. The two younger shepherds looked cautiously about the room, then stood outside, as if on guard. The third looked into the wrinkled face of the woman.

"Please. We are in great need of your help."

The woman glanced at the old master. His smiling face seemed noncommittal.

"What could I do to help you?" asked the ancient woman as she played with a golden ring on her crooked finger. The king noticed that the ring was shaped as a serpent swallowing its tail.

"Do you have special sight into things touching on the Blue Planet and beyond?"

"Father, you must be mistaken. None who do such things live in the New Land. The king ordered all such men and women put to death."

The old master spoke up. "It is certain that none with power are in danger in this circle, and my friends are not so poor as might appear."

To show that the old man spoke truth, the oldest shepherd drew a hand from his cloak. He held a small bag and opened its drawstring to reveal pieces of silver and gold and jewelry. The woman looked in astonishment at the wealth, then eyed the men and relaxed.

"I see who you are," she said with a smile.

The disguised king stiffened. "Who are we?"

"With your strong friends outside, I am sure you have relieved many travelers of their riches, but that is not my concern. Shall we begin?"

One hanging lamp was left burning. It cast splashes of light as the woman of darkness danced about with the lithe movements of a dancing girl. Her movements were slow, then she whirled faster and faster, chanting slithery, snakelike syllables. Now she spun so quickly that she seemed one with the light. Suddenly she froze, her eyes closed and her face pointing upward toward the light. With monotone words as from sleep, she asked: "What ancient soul from beyond Blue Planet do you wish?"

"I must hear the words of Speaker," said the king.

The woman had not even begun her incantations when a voice boomed out. It seemed to come from the walls themselves.

"What words would you have me say, you foolish king?!"

The voice came out of nowhere, and an image of an old man with a long, white beard and angry eyes appeared.

"I see that you at last have taken the final step in showing how much you despise King-Maker."

"I am in great distress," cried out the king. "The warriors of the sea are vast beyond our strength. And the voice of King-Maker is silent. I must know how to get his help to save myself and my kingdom."

"Why should King-Maker save you and your kingdom? He will not. You have seen your last sunset. When the sun lights the Mountains of the Dawn. . .

"you will fall to the sword,

"and your sons will fall to the sword,

"and your army will know bitter loss."

The image faded and First King collapsed. The woman had been cringing on the floor in terror, but now she regained her composure. She collapsed onto a stool and looked on as First King's bodyguards revived him.

"Am I right that this man is First King?" she asked quietly. "What does he need?"

"He has pushed himself many hours without food."

"Let him rest on my bed, while I prepare something to give strength," said the witch. "But I must know: Will he order my death when he comes to himself?"

First King stirred.

"Kind woman, you are safe from my hand," he murmured.

The witch quickly killed a goat and mixed portions of the choicest meats with vegetables for a stew. She set out wine. The king in rags ate until his strength was renewed.

"The morning light will come in a few hours. We must go quickly," the king said. He gave the woman the bag of gold. Her hand hesitated to take it.

"You know," she said, "that I had little to do with what happened here tonight. I fear a curse accompanies these things."

"You deserve death for dabbling in the dark ways of Shining One," the king said. "Therein lies the curse, not in this money. Take it and follow King-Maker. The curse this night is on me."

First King got slowly to his feet. "Now I and my family and my men must face it."

With a cry the Army of the Kingdom plunged toward the waiting People of the Sea. Bowmen sent volley after volley into the flanks where men and chariots waited. Arrows also rained down on the charging line. Men could not run and hold their shields above them, so many fell. Outnumbered as they were, they could not flank the enemy. A hammering frontal assault designed to split the Sea People's line at its weakest point was the only practical strategy. Bowmen and slingmen held back to try to beat off the chariot assault that would slice through from the sides.

The Sea People hoped to end this fight quickly. The Kingdom Army would not hold without First King.

Up and down the line the word had gone out: "Look for the king and press the attack directly at him. Kill the king!"

The clash of battle was deafening. The strength of the Sea People's Army was overwhelming. The king's guard fled to a more defensible hillside where chariots were less maneuverable, but the foot soldiers' attack was unstoppable.

"To the king!" yelled Prince. Three of First King's sons stepped between their father and those who wished him dead. They circled their father with their shields and stood firm against a thousand bows. They defended the king with the courage of the hopeless. A wound to the neck felled one. A thrust to the side sent another reeling. The mighty prince fought on. Eight, nine, ten men fell to his sword before a tendon was severed in his shoulder. Eleven, twelve, thirteen lay before him when a thrust found his cheek and then his belly.

A soldier struck on the left.

Two struck on the right.

Three made the final frontal assault.

Prince finally went to his knees as a large warrior let out a blood-stopping cry and swung his sword with a terrifying force.

A few steps away the king dropped to the ground. Blood soaked into the leather of his armor. He felt the strength ebb from his body.

The young man who bore his shield stood fearlessly at his side.

"Come close," First King said with great effort. "Come close and draw your sword."

"Yes, my king," said the boy. "What shall I do?"

"Drive it through my heart."

"No, my king, I cannot harm you."

"If they capture me, they will torture and mock and then kill me."

But the armor-bearer refused.

First King set his sword's grip in the ground. He placed the point at his heart and whispered, "Oh, King-Maker, forgive me for disappointing you. Bless the Shepherd King."

He fell on his sword. The young bearer of the king's shield looked at the dying man before him and at the fallen spread across the battlefield. Panic gripped his heart and he drew his sword and fell on its point.

The death of their king was indeed the final blow to the People of the Promise. Survivors scattered to the hills. The battle was over and the land was cut in two. Half the enemy army marched north and the other half marched south. The soldiers of the sea claimed each city as their own.

The bodies of First King and his three sons were dragged from the battlefield. The head of the king was displayed before the temple of Shining One. The royal bodies were hung at the center of a nearby village, while the victorious soldiers walked by and spit upon them.

Valiant warriors from the east bank of the Winding River learned of the outrage and journeyed through the night. They took down the four bodies in the darkness and carried them away for secret burial

in a deserted place,

on a windswept hill,

beneath an ancient tamarisk tree.

Their graves were unmarked and unknown, except by the warriors who laid the empty forms into the dust of the New Land.

NO TRUE KINGDOM
IS BUILT QUICKLY
OR WITHOUT COST.

CHAPTER 8

THE SHEPHERD KING

I have come from the Valley of Harvests," said the tired messenger, who was covered with dirt and blood. "The Army of the Kingdom is no more. Our living soldiers hide with the foxes. The Sea People walk our lands unhindered."

Shepherd had taken refuge in the land of the Sea People. He knew the invasion plans and the certain results. He turned away from the messenger and his officers.

Could he stop his ears and not hear the rest? He knew the judgment of King-Maker. If only it were not so.

"What of First King? And what of his sons?"

"They fell fighting bravely together on a battle-torn hillside."

"This is certain?" asked Shepherd with a shudder.

"I saw the enemy press around them. I heard the shouts of triumph."

The army was crushed, the kingdom fallen. A cry rose from the throat of Shepherd, until all the camp heard the news. Each one knew someone who had fought and died that day—friends or brothers or fathers. The camp took up the cry. They mourned and wept and fasted.

With an ache in his heart and tears in his eyes, Shepherd called for his lyre. Numb fingers played a haunting tune and pain-filled words poured forth: "The mighty ones have fallen.

"They were swifter than eagles,

"and stronger than lions,

"and more beautiful than graceful gazelles."

As he searched for words, Shepherd thought of Prince and his brothers, the royal sons. He remembered his music for the king. If only that man had followed King-Maker.

Words for his song came out as sobs.

In the last light of day, his men gathered to listen to the lament. They thought of those who had fought with First King. Even those sent to hunt them were countrymen and comrades. So many had fallen; so many lay broken in the Valley of Harvest.

Together they sang songs of loss and sorrow and tragedy for the kingdom. They looked beyond the sky and asked for mercy. They asked that they might be part of a new kingdom with Shepherd as their new king.

For a cycle of the moon Shepherd mourned. Then he walked the highlands with King-Maker, pouring out his fears and hopes and dreams:

"My enemy is dead and I am now the anointed king. But my kingdom is oppressed. What shall I do?"

"Go to your people," said the wind.

"Where shall I start?"

"Go to the Valley of Apples and the tribe of your father."

So Shepherd and his mighty warriors journeyed to the Valley of Apples. Word of their coming spread and a large, joyful group greeted their arrival. People crowded the road and cheered and cried: "Long live the Shepherd King."

Messengers were sent to the tribal elders of the southern tribes. Within days the great men of the lands gathered in the beautiful valley. Shepherd knelt and they confirmed the decision of King-Maker by anointing him with olive oil flecked with gold. Golden glitter sparkled on his head and beard.

A representative for the elders spoke to Shepherd and all those gathered:

"From this day you are Shepherd King," he shouted. "The one beyond the sky has planted your name in our hearts. Follow his steps and we will follow you."

Shepherd King lifted his head and shouted so that all could hear him:

"Our land is divided.

"An enemy holds us captive.

"North and South are two peoples.

"But there will shine a day when our enemy staggers and all our brothers join hands. The New Land will again smile upon a united kingdom."

In the north, the last surviving son of First King was crowned to continue his father's dynasty. The New Land was now under the oppression of an invader and headed by two kings. Long animosities between North and South broke into armed skirmishes, and sometimes fierce battles. The feuding brothers bickered and fought, threatened and fought, boasted and fought.

But the rule of Shepherd King grew wiser and stronger and prosperous, while First King's son grew weaker and weaker. He had not learned the ways of kings. He was, after all, the youngest son. True rule fell to the powerful commander of the northern army.

So First King's son turned faint when he learned the dreadful news that his advisor and regent had been struck down in battle. The man hid in his house, for he did not know how to bring together the pieces of his crumbling crown. His people lost faith in him. They remembered the one man who had led them with courage and confidence—the one who had never been defeated in battle, even in personal combat against Giant. They remembered that they had not always fought their southern brothers. Once they had turned their swords against a common enemy. The king did not realize that his kingdom had turned against him. The people's love was no more.

One day as the sun burned its hottest, the Northern King rested alone in his sleeping room. In the house were two of his closest friends, brothers who had commanded successful raids into the south. They were guests at his table. It was customary for the king to host friends and relatives each day. But this day the brothers did not want food. They wanted the life of their king. In his chamber they found the king asleep on his bed. They stabbed him and cut off his head before his death agonies roused others. They slipped from the house and traveled south to the Valley of Apples. The thanks of Shepherd King would be lavish.

"Shepherd King," they said with great respect, "we bring you the son of First King." The pale head of death was presented. The king turned away in disgust.

The brothers were surprised at his reaction: "The northern tribes now have no leader. You will be welcomed as you come to unite the kingdom."

"This is your work?" asked the king.

"Our swords are ever at your command."

"You have done me no favor," Shepherd King said in anger. "The nation will believe that I stained my hands with the blood of an innocent man in his own home."

"Most will not care. You are the rightful king."

The audience was not going as they hoped. Guards were ordered to bind them.

"You murdered a defenseless man asleep in the comfort of his bed. You stained your hands and mine with royal blood. You have called forth the judgment of King-Maker. Your days are ended!"

Leaders of the North who came to the Valley of Apples the next day could see a gruesome sight—the suspended bodies of executed murderers. Assured that Shepherd King was blameless and the killers had found justice, they asked Shepherd to accept the crown of all the People of Promise:

"Shepherd our people.

"Unite our two kingdoms.

"Drive out our enemies."

A disciple of the Speaker placed the golden crown upon his head in the name of the one above all. The New Land was again under a strong king. There was hope. The kingdom looked to one who looked beyond the sky.

King-Maker smiled.

Word soon reached the king of the People of the Sea. How had his plan to keep the parts of the kingdom divided against each other come to nothing? Danger was before him.

"Send every warrior at our disposal out now. We must kill the new king before he has time to draw together an army."

Shepherd King of the Sea People thought he could not be conquered. He forgot that the soldiers of his enemy had been fighting one another for years and so were well trained. Nor did he take into account that the one who gave breath to all would fight for his people once more.

Shepherd King had a quiet confidence as his runners spread through the kingdom, and the armies of North and South gathered to learn to fight together instead of killing one another.

Swiftly the battle-hardened warriors moved toward the Army of the Sea People. They collided. The soldiers of the sea were driven back. They regrouped and struck again. Where had this enemy gotten its strength? They fought with the vision of a homeland under Shepherd and King-Maker.

The Sea People finally retreated to their border, beaten and humiliated and frightened.

"Our enemy is defeated! We are free! We are a nation," cheered the people. Joy and celebration spread across the country.

Shepherd King was ready to take the next step.

"We will never be truly united while I rule from either of the old capitals of North and South," he told the elders. "We are a new people in the New Land. We need a new city separate from the past."

He knew where that city should be—the ancient City of Palms. So strong was this city, however, that it had never been wrestled from the stubborn followers of Shining One. They still lived as neighbors, uneasily coexisting with the People of Promise.

To Shepherd King this was an opportunity as well as an obstacle. His united army would build a united capital in a city that had been neither North nor South. And an enemy of King-Maker would be destroyed.

So the army marched on the City of Palms. Most of the soldiers feared they were approaching an unconquerable fortress. On three sides steep ravines made an assault suicide. Thick walls around the city were especially tall on the north side—the only logical point of attack.

Leaders of the city who stood atop the north wall were confident.

"Go home," they yelled. "This fortress shall never be yours. Not even King-Maker could conquer this citadel."

Shepherd ordered half his warriors to scale the massive walls with climbing hooks. Attentions diverted, the defenders did not notice that other soldiers were gathering about a bubbling spring east of the city. There Shepherd King knew he would find secret tunnels that channeled water into the very heart of the fortress.

Before light died, the unconquerable citadel was in Shepherd King's hands. He declared it capital of the New Land and moved his family within its walls.

The wise king of the Northern Coastlands was delighted that the civil war was over and his enemies the Sea People put down. He congratulated Shepherd King and sent skilled workmen as a gift. They would build a magnificent palace of cedar and stone.

More important than a palace was the home of the Ark of Mystery, ancient symbol of the relationship between King-Maker and his people. It was stored in the back room of a dwelling miles away.

"The Ark of Mystery must be moved to our new capital," declared Shepherd. "It is the throne of King-Maker."

Thousands gathered along the route the ark would take. No onlooker was old enough to have seen the Ark of Mystery, but all knew its importance. Men descended from the keepers of the Special Place slowly carried the majestic box that had been shamefully ignored during the reign of First King.

All marveled at the two golden angels facing each other with out-stretched wings. They dreamed of its history and the powerful tokens of the past it contained:

Two stone tablets with ten words;

A golden jar of morning bread;

A shepherd's staff from which flowers had bloomed.

With music and singing and dancing, the Ark of Mystery was moved to the City of Palms. Rams' horns blasted. Men and women and children cheered as the Ark entered the city walls. Awaiting it was the Special Place that had been built in the desert to house it. The flat-roofed tent was made with the finest linen of blue and purple and scarlet, embroidered with angels.

Shepherd entered the tent with his head bent and sacrificed a spotless, newborn lamb to the one who is infinite and eternal and all-powerful. A new kind of kingdom had begun, a kingdom such as the world had never known.

In the Special Place, Shepherd King poured out his heart in a song to King-Maker: "You are so good and I am so small. Yet you have blessed me. . .

"beyond what I deserve

"or have sought

"or have dreamed."

A soft wind rustled the curtains. "Walk close to me and your joy will overflow. Walk away and you will know sorrow."

The king bowed, thanking the maker of all for his kingdom and crown and contentment.

"Help me walk close to you each day."

CHAPTER 9

THE BEGUILING BEAUTY

The feel of walls and floor; the smell of cedar—after years on the run, living in tents and caves and under the stars, the fine palace seemed an amazing place. Its craftsmen were sent home to the king of the Northern Coastlands with the richest gifts of thanks Shepherd King and his impoverished nation could afford.

The kingdom was a toddling infant, weak and full of promise. Now the threat was from desert raiders. To protect his people, Shepherd King would have to take the offensive to the very walls of the capital of the Plains People.

But he was tired. He needed to learn how to rule, rather than chase around the country at the head of an army. And how could he leave his new home? His nephew would command in his place.

So in the spring, when kings went off to war, Shepherd King walked the first miles with his army. Then he waved farewell and returned to the comforts of his palace. He knew his motives were not pure. He knew he should turn and catch up with his troops. He almost did.

The army journeyed toward the dawn, crossed the Winding River. There they encountered a large force on its way to the New Land to taste and steal the first harvest. The raiders retreated to the City of Springs. This fortress at the headwaters of the Falling River had tall, strong walls. The capital of the Plains People would not fall easily. The army settled in for a siege —occasional fierce battles interspersed with mind-numbing monotony. It was better than the hunger inside the walls—but not much.

Shepherd King used his time receiving elders from villages and whole tribes. Problems were solved. Strong connections were forged. Shepherd King also worked with architects and builders on enlarging his city walls, no small undertaking in a city built upon a mountain.

With such a flurry of activity, the king was often exhausted. He frequently was too tired for walks in the highlands with King-Maker. King-Maker would understand.

In the evenings he relaxed on his fine flat roof and watched the city below. In the cool of the day when shadows grew long, Shepherd King paced the rooftop of his magnificent palace. Here he asked King-Maker to protect his men and give them victory. As the world faded to orange-dipped gray and the first oil lamps were lit, he noticed the activities on rooftops down the mountain. On one a mother and father rolled a wooden toy to a toddler who reached out chubby hands to grasp at it. A keeper of the Special Place faced the departing sun and held out his arms to King-Maker in thanksgiving.

A shapely young woman stepped from the shadows and began letting her long hair down. Servants poured water into a large earthenware bowl. They withdrew and the woman slipped from her clothing and began to wash the day's heat from her body. The sight was intimate and the woman beautiful.

The next day Shepherd King could not keep his mind on matters brought before him. But he gazed in rapt attention as the scene was repeated on the second and third and fourth twilights. Her alabaster body shimmered in the flickering flames of a lamp. His heart beat fast as she moved so slowly and gracefully and enchantingly.

The king called a servant and asked, "Who is the woman who lives alone below us?"

"She is a granddaughter of your chief advisor."

This family had been with him in the wilderness. Now he recalled the little girl he had watched play. The child was grown. One of his most beloved officers, a foreigner who had come to follow King-Maker, had excitedly told him of betrothal to this girl. That had been years ago.

"She is the wife of one of your most loyal officers," the servant said, answering the unasked question.

"She is probably lonely and would like to see the palace," Shepherd King reasoned. "Ask her to dine with me tomorrow as darkness falls."

The king and the young woman ate a sumptuous meal, attended by discreet servants. They spoke of mutual friends and past times. She was charming and shy and respectful. After eating, they stood looking out over the city laid out before them.

"I can see many things from this roof."

She looked at him demurely. "Yes, I know."

"I can see your rooftop. I have seen you there."

"Yes, I know."

"You are the most beautiful of women. My whole being cries out to hold you and feel your softness next to me."

"You know I am married. I have enjoyed your admiring looks and attentions, but we cannot go on."

"But we must," he said and brought her close.

She did not pull away. Passion drowned reason and propriety and the ways of King-Maker.

Lips caressed.

Bodies touched.

Vows were broken.

Alone she slipped from the palace. The excitement of the night had turned to shame and a touch of fear. A cycle of the moon passed and she sent word to her king: "A new life has begun in me."

Shepherd paced and pondered. He too felt shame. His hunger for her was not satisfied, but he wished he had looked the other way when the lovely silhouette let down her hair.

He had assumed their adventure would remain hidden. Now that seemed impossible.

What would her husband do?

What would her father say?

What would all the people think?

"You can bury this secret," hissed a large snake nearby.

"Who are you?" asked the king.

"Once I was most beautiful of all the angels. Now I rule the Blue Planet."

"You are Shining One," said Shepherd. "You have no power, for King-Maker holds everything in his hands."

"Yes, but much slips through his fingers. You have power enough for this small matter," hissed the snake. "Your problem is that the husband has not been with his wife. So bring them together. Then who is to know that he did not bring forth this new life?"

"The answer is so simple," the king realized. Immediately a runner went out.

The king stepped forward and grasped his warrior's shoulders. Despite the expression of warmth, the king seemed distant. "You have been my valiant warrior," said Shepherd. "I honor you and call you to go home. Rest and spend time with your wife. Then I will send you back with papers for your commander."

"I am glad I please you, but I do all for the one who holds the stars in his hands."

Late that night the king received a message from the woman: "My husband has not come to me."

He was found the next morning, asleep on the ground outside the palace.

"Why didn't you obey me?" demanded the king.

"My comrades eat stale bread and sleep in open fields. How could I enjoy myself?"

"Stay another day," said the king. "Tomorrow I will send you back."

That night the soldier attended a banquet. He ate his fill of lamb and bread and fruit. He drank the most intoxicating wine. Servants kept his cup full. He stumbled from the banquet, and servants helped him toward his house. But again he refused. The next day he was found asleep on the ground outside the palace gate.

"Men like this are beyond reasoning," said the snake. "There is only one course of action. He cannot return home to find new life growing large inside his wife."

"I will find another way."

"There is no other way. And if you hesitate, all the kingdom will know. In his dishonor, her husband will demand revenge."

Still groggy from all the wine, the soldier began the walk back to battle. He gave scrolls to the commander, who broke the seals and looked thoughtfully at the document. The king ordered that he plan a battle that would be lost, a battle whose only design was to kill one of his finest men? What was this madness?

A plan was made and valiant soldiers stormed the City of Springs. A small force led by the doomed warrior was to lead the way, carrying a great timber to ram the massive gates. The attack seemed ill-conceived, but perhaps the commander had learned of a weakness. So the soldiers charged with all their will. Archers atop the lofty stone walls let loose a shower of deadly shafts. As the warriors of King-Maker held high their shields against the arrows, the gates swung open. Plains soldiers flooded out of the city to meet their charge.

The faithful warriors at the gate faced their hopeless situation with unflinching resolve. "Sharpen my weapon and strengthen my arm," the fine warrior asked King-Maker, then he and the others met and slowed the charging enemy before they were cut down.

"He is dead. The truth lies buried on a battlefield," hissed Shining One to Shepherd King.

"Leave me alone," cried the king in grief and anguish and remorse.

The fallen soldiers were mourned. The weeping king spoke of courage, and many new widows wept bitter tears. But as soon as her eyes had dried, Shepherd King brought the widow of the valiant leader of the warriors to the palace. There were whispers, but none spoke aloud.

Only King-Maker.

One of the keepers of the Special Place was a trusted advisor to the king, and a truth-teller who listened carefully and walked closely with King-Maker. One morning the man asked to see the king. He was in a most agitated state.

"I have just learned of a great crime. Two men live in your kingdom, one in great wealth and one in utter poverty. The rich man has many sheep and cattle and donkeys that grace his vast landholdings. But he has stolen the poor man's only possession, a tiny lamb that he cherished. It was taken and slaughtered because the wealthy man needed a roasted lamb quickly for a visitor. It was served on a silver platter."

This story had great effect on Shepherd King. How could anyone do such a thing? "The wealthy man deserves to die," he shouted. "Tell me his name, and he will be severely punished."

The truth-teller summoned his courage and looked into the eyes of the king.

"His name is Shepherd. You are the evil man. You have betrayed a faithful warrior and a trusting nation and the king over all kings."

Shepherd's face was ashen.

His body went limp.

His soul ached.

He fell to the floor and covered his face and cried out to King-Maker: "I have declared it. I stand condemned. My sorrow is beyond words. I ask nothing but your mercy—

"Wash away my darkness.

"Purify my heart.

"Break me, but do not leave me."

The king let out a pained wail: "My sorrow is beyond words." He did not look up when the truth-teller laid a hand on his shoulder.

"Most evildoers are sorry that they have been caught. You are sorry because you intimately love the one that you have offended. There is hope for you. In years to come you will wish you had faced the executioner. This child will die in your place. But you are washed by an eternal love."

From his birth the son was very weak. Many spotless, newborn lambs were sacrificed. Shepherd King prayed that the curse on his child's body would rest on him instead. But the tiny one was too fragile for life on the Blue Planet.

A summer and a winter passed and again spring's harvests touched the New Land. The widow of the brave warrior again felt new life within her. When her second son was born the kingdom danced.

Shepherd, the humbled king, walked the highlands in the misty mornings before the sun rose over the Mountains of the Dawn. The wind washed away his darkness with a special promise of the child who had been born:

"This is a child of peace.

"He shall rule with wisdom.

"And your throne will be established forever."

GRASPING FOR MORE
REQUIRES LETTING GO
OF WHAT IS FIRMLY IN HAND.

CHAPTER 10

THE REBEL

The maiden lay in the street, her breathing ragged, her robe of fine fabric torn and dirty. Tears pushed through the dust covering her bruised face to form rivers of mourning. No veil covered her, as was proper for a maiden. Nothing was proper here. This was no woman of the streets who wailed in the dust, but one of regal loveliness.

So people stared and pointed, but none stopped.

A young nobleman looked at her curiously. "I know who she is," he whispered with a start, then turned and walked quickly toward the higher city.

The young woman pulled herself painfully to her feet. There was a commotion of running feet as servants following the young man arrived. Women servants supported her as she walked slowly back up the street. Even now onlookers surmised that they had seen something dark and dirty and blasphemous. The maiden noticed their looks. She pushed back from her helpers, straightened, and limped off on her own. At the door of the wing of the palace reserved for royal women, she collapsed.

Soon a handsome young man demanded entrance from the doorkeepers and approached her bedside. "Oh, my sister," he whispered in grief as he saw her tangled hair and swollen eyes. "Water!" he called.

As he moistened her face and wiped away tears her story was told amid broken sobs.

"Our brother did this," she began.

"What has he done?" the man demanded.

"He looked on me in desire. He tricked me into coming to him. He. . .tore my clothing and did with me all he wished and threw me out into the street. What will I do, brother? No man will want me now, and I

70

can no longer stay among the women of the king."

"You will stay in my home," the young man decided quickly, "and we shall see that the king rights this evil. I vow that he will hear of it before the moon rises this day."

He did hear all. Shepherd King faced two staggering losses. His tender daughter had been abused most hideously and his own son had committed the crime. In any village the elders would condemn him to die at the hands of the people. His eldest was brutal and selfish and wild.

"My son had all he could wish, but look what he has done."

In his anger he considered his own past—saw images of a woman letting down her hair in the dying light of day. Could he condemn this son, when he had killed to cover his own behavior?

So the guilt of the father paralyzed the justice of the king. He knew not what to do, so he did nothing. His inaction justified his son. Judges would not move in difficult matters if the king would not, and violence infected all. It was not that people didn't care. But administering justice was hard and painful and unrewarding. Without the model of just leadership, problems went unsolved. The oldest son of the king walked the streets as if innocent, while his sister hid in shadows.

Her younger brother paced the courtyard of his home. His grieving spirit festered. Why did his father not act? Admiration for the king turned to bitter disappointment and resentment and hatred. The son came to be known as Rebel.

Time passed.

The eldest son did not suspect danger when a feast was provided by Rebel for all the brothers. But his death was an obsession to Rebel—

wrong for wrong,

violence for violence,

evil for evil.

All the king's sons received the invitation: "It has been a good year. Many lambs were born. The wool is thick and long, and shearing is almost over. Celebrate with me by the City of Palms."

The feast was set out in a remote meadow. Such a meal even the king's sons had seldom seen. They ate and drank and became merry.

Rebel stood before them.

"Brothers," he said, "This is a day to remember. I only wish our dear sister were here, but she does not leave the shelter of my roof. She will not see her vindication, which has come at last."

Before any could react, strong men lifted the oldest brother from where he reclined to eat.

His arms were held.

A hidden sword was drawn.

The soil received blood.

In the midst of the anarchy, Rebel raised his goblet: "Let all know that my sister is innocent. The guilty one has been punished."

Word of the murder left Shepherd King shocked and numb and aching. He ordered that Rebel be brought before him. But Rebel was in a place of hiding, far from the City of Palms. For three summers he hid, while his sister was an able steward for his property and herds.

One day the king walked with his nephew, the commander.

"You seem preoccupied," said the nephew.

"I was thinking of Rebel. He is a good man, who acted more justly than did I."

"Yes, even King-Maker's law allows revenge by a brother in a just cause."

"But Rebel is ambitious. I fear he will seek my throne."

"Then by all means allow him to return so he is close—where you can watch him. Even now it is said that you keep him far away out of fear."

So Shepherd King sent messengers who announced that Rebel was pardoned. Rebel purchased a white donkey, such as kings rode, and entered the City of Palms as if he were its conqueror. He was forgiven, but he did not forgive. Plans were made and conspirators gathered and the respect of the people nurtured. The work required the passing of summers, but Rebel was a patient man.

When all was ready, Rebel journeyed south to rally his supporters. Already he was more popular than his father. With the kingdom in hand, the hearts of the people would follow. Leaders of the nation were summoned to see Rebel crowned king in the Valley of Apples. Some pledged their allegiance. Others remained faithful to Shepherd King but went home afraid.

Rams' horns sounded.

The news was announced.

Celebrations broke out across the kingdom.

The nation's leaders well knew that Rebel plotted, but the suddenness and completeness of his victory was startling. "The hearts of the people are with your son," came a report from the Valley of Apples.

"Rebel has an army, led by the commander of First King. Soldiers who loved First King have gathered around him," came another.

"We can hold the city but at the cost of many lives. Brother will attack brother. Neighbor will kill neighbor as they lay siege to their own capital. No, I will give my throne to Rebel before I allow that. We must flee."

The city was deathly still as the procession of servants and bodyguards and warriors followed carts loaded with provisions through the great northern gate. They traveled through a winding valley and past olive groves on the eastern ridge. They looked back on their own abandoned homes and wondered if they would ever return.

Atop the ridge, Shepherd stood beside his donkey, gazing at the distant city. When a friend stopped, the king pointed sadly to the far distance.

"Look," he said sadly.

A large force was approaching the gates, which stood open and waiting, presided over by one of Shepherd King's oldest friends and advisors.

"They have come so quickly."

"They thought to catch us before we escaped," said the king. "They nearly did."

"We are trapped if they come after us now."

Shepherd King nodded. "We have two allies, the one above all and the one who has been left behind. I trust my kingdom to these confederates."

In the city Rebel stood with his two chief advisors. "With the capital under our control, what shall we do?" asked Rebel of his first advisor, who had been chief counselor to Shepherd King for many years. However, this advisor had remained at Shepherd's side only to gain revenge. His granddaughter was the beautiful woman whose husband had been killed to cover the king's crime. He had never forgiven the king. His heart was bitter and his dreams danced with revenge.

"Only hours ago your enemy stood on this spot," he said gleefully. "They are few and weak and dispirited. Send your warriors to trap Shepherd King before he reaches the Winding River."

"Your plan is bold," Rebel said.

He turned to his other advisor, whose presence in the city had been unexpected. This counselor had served Shepherd King faithfully. His defection was a boon.

"What do you say?"

"Were we facing any other king I would agree. But you face a desert wolf who has prevailed against superior odds many times. He knows this ground, and his men will fight like demons. Such a veteran fighter might set a trap. If the victory is not total, the people will doubt you."

Rebel nodded thoughtfully. "Your counsel?"

"You own the people. Make this their battle as well as your own. Gather mighty men from throughout the kingdom. Build your forces until they are numerous as the sand by the sea. Shepherd King will be the outlaw once more. All will join to crush him."

The young man stood and thought for a moment.

"Your course seems the wiser. I have come this far by acting carefully. I should not be precipitous now. I will do as you say and act when I am certain."

His first advisor turned gray.

"If you make this choice I believe you will lose everything."

As night approached, a lone palace servant slipped through a side gate and hurried north toward the fleeing followers of Shepherd. His message for the king: "I have gained time for you to cross the Winding River and gather your forces. May King-Maker stand at your side until you return in peace and victory."

At about the same time, the first advisor slowly slipped through the main gates on his donkey and took the south road toward his home. Hours later in the midst of the night he reached the house of his father and his father's father, the house where he had taken his first steps and studied his first books. Now he prepared a clay tablet and picked up his stylus.

"Please try to understand.

"I turned against my king, and all is lost.

"Forgive me."

He gave instructions concerning all that he owned. And as the blue shadows of dawn gave way to the yellow rays of sun his body was found hanging from the heavy beams of his ceiling.

Shepherd King and his followers crossed the Winding River and pushed east to the Falling River. Crowds who lined the road gave respect and gifts. Finally Shepherd King reached a haven where he might gather an army and ready his plan for the decisive battle.

Rebel also sent messengers to gather mighty men to his side. When he believed his force invincible, he crossed the Winding River.

"Bring to me the head of the man who gave me life," he told his commanders. "Only then can my throne be safe."

Shepherd King had a very different message: "Fight a good fight. Return me to my kingdom. But be gentle with my son."

The armies came together in a woodland south of Falling River. Blood splattered the underbrush.

As the sun settled toward the western horizon, the general outcome was clear. The army of Rebel was neither as prepared nor as passionate as those who longed to return their king to his throne. The hand of King-Maker strengthened the arms of Shepherd King.

Rebel had lost, but perhaps this was but a setback in his design. He mounted his mule and fled through tree and thicket to escape his father's army. He left the main trail at a gallop, hoping to lose his father's forces. But the mule was moving too fast and the branches were too low. One of them swept him from his mount. From the branch that had caught him he hung, swinging by his hair, barely conscious and bereft even of a sword. Soon he was surrounded by enemy soldiers.

"Let's kill him and go home to our families," a warrior shouted.

"No!" answered another. "We must spare his life."

A messenger was sent to the commander for orders.

"It is unfortunate that he did not fall in the heat of battle," said the commander. "I will come and take responsibility in this."

The commander was brought to the giant oak where Rebel still struggled. Without hesitation, he thrust a spear through Rebel's heart. The body was cast into a pit and stones heaped over it. Then the commander sent a messenger, who threw himself onto the ground before the king.

"Rejoice, for King-Maker has rescued you from all who rose against you."

With a gesture the king swept aside news of his victory. He looked at the messenger earnestly. "What of Rebel? What of my son?"

"Never again will he rise against you."

The wail of a breaking heart was heard through the camp. "My son!

My beloved! You paid the penalty for pride and rebellion. But it was truly my pride and my rebellion that stole your life. King-Maker, take my life and end this cycle of pain I cause."

Only Shepherd heard the distant voice echoing through the blood-drenched wood: "You have fought well this day. Look beyond the sky and listen to my words and walk always in my ways."

ACCEPTING RESPONSIBILITY FOR FAILURE
OPENS THE DOOR TO BOTH CONSEQUENCE AND GRACE.

CHAPTER 11

THE NUMBERING

The great rebellion begun by Rebel was at an end and it was time to go home. It had taken time and stern words from the commander of his army, but at last the king had stopped mourning for his dead son. The hearts of the people lifted when they saw his crown glitter in the afternoon sun. Shepherd smiled, for he saw a goodness in his people.

He led his followers south through the forests and west across the Winding River. They moved through the highlands to the gates of the City of Palms. Feasting had already begun within the walls. That night the king slept peacefully within his magnificent palace.

But peace was not to last long. A nobleman from the tribe of First King was named Trouble. Though he remembered little of the years under First King, he longed to return the crown to his tribe. So he conspired with others of like mind and gathered the northern tribes around him. They refused to submit to Shepherd King and another uprising began.

Shepherd King had taken the army from the old commander, for he had learned the facts of the death of his son. He made his nephew commander, charging him to settle this threat quickly. This new commander had courage in battle, but he believed that the only certain way not to lose battles was not to fight them. He ordered and trained and prepared but refused to break camp. Finally the exasperated king sent for the old commander to bring the army to action.

Near the City of Palms the kinsmen commanders met. The old approached the new with a smile and embrace. But inside he seethed with rage for his lost position. To take out his anger against Shepherd King was a fool's revenge, and the commander had not become a great military leader by being a fool. This young commander was at the heart of the injustice. All this the old commander remembered as he embraced his young kinsman—slipping the dagger from his belt and plunging it deep into the body of his rival.

"Throw this body off of the road," shouted the old commander to his men. "Now let us deal with anyone who stands against the king."

Trouble and his inexperienced army did not understand the ways of battle. Soon they were cornered, forced to take refuge behind the walls of a fortified city at the headwaters of the Winding River. The king's men surrounded the city and laid siege.

From the wall's edge above the gate a woman hailed the army. She called to speak with the commander.

"Why are you trying to destroy us?" asked the woman. "We are a peaceful people, and you are our kinsmen."

"If you have not sided against your king, we mean you no harm," the commander shouted back. "But an enemy lies within your walls, one who threatens the kingdom. Hand him over and we will leave you with our thanks. We want no innocent blood on our swords."

The wise woman was an elder of the city. She and the other elders called Trouble to meet with them.

"You certainly fit your name," they said to him. "You have brought great trouble to this city. We have protected you at the hazard of our lives, but we have not learned the reasons you stand against the government of Shepherd King. Please, join us in private. We will drink wine together and speak of these things."

After the meeting the elder woman summoned all the rebel war band to assemble in the marketplace.

"Brothers," she said. "Your coming has brought our city into danger, and your own lives will be lost if the great army at our gates gains entry. We have given you shelter as our kinsmen but not as your allies. Your leader has explained your quarrel with the king. But as he took wine with us he suddenly became sick and sank down to the floor and we are unable to revive him. So now you are left with no leader and an enemy who will destroy you if you do not submit.

"Perhaps we should make peace, and I can send this army on their way."

A short while later the woman again stood above the gate. Again she summoned the commander to the gate. She tossed down a bloodstained bag. He bent down to look inside and quietly closed it and listened as she spoke.

"Behold, the man you sought. As you can see, he no longer is a threat to our king. We have looked and can find no other rebels within the city walls. If you wish you may come into our city, but you will find none in arms against you. It would seem that your business is accomplished."

"Yes, it does seem so," answered the commander. "Your city is blessed by King-Maker with prudent leaders. I leave you with Shepherd King's blessing."

The commander blew his ram's horn and the army returned to the king.

Again there was peace throughout the land, but the king remained cautious. An inner voice reminded him that neighboring nations had watched his struggles. They were looking for an opportunity to crush his kingdom. From what direction would the next threat arise?

"King-Maker is our protector," he reminded himself. "He is our sword and shield and strength. If an enemy rises against us, He will lead us to victory."

"But victory also requires warriors," answered the inner voice, spoken in his ear with a snakelike hiss. "You have failed King-Maker."

"How have I failed the one above all?"

"You cannot ably rule King-Maker's great kingdom if you don't know how many warriors you can call to battle. Your crown is a trust and you are failing it."

Shepherd looked to the wind. "Does King-Maker truly wish to have me number my men?" asked Shepherd. "Surely he knows the number of all armies."

The serpentine voice again whispered inside his head. The breeze was silent.

"You have led your people for many years. Must King-Maker tell you everything? He has anointed you as the leader of his vast people. Every great king numbers his people. Would he have you do less?"

All night he pondered the words.

"I believe we should learn the number of our able-bodied fighting men," he told his advisors the next day. "We must be ready to stand against the threats around us. Send men through the land and count every soldier who can raise a sword in battle."

When Shepherd King saw the numbers he was amazed at how many stood at his command. Immediately his heart swelled with pride.

In the darkest part of the night his heart became troubled. Sleep would not come. In desperation he looked beyond the sky and cried out: "Have I followed your voice or the voice of another?"

"You know the answer," breathed the wind. "Have I ever asked you to trust in your own strength instead of mine? You have listened to the voice of your pride, which is a dangerous thing for a king to do. Pride is the tool of Shining One. He has used it to cause many to fall."

Early the next morning a keeper of the Special Place stood before the palace. The king quickly gave him entrance.

"I have not listened to the words of King-Maker," said the king with his head bent. "I have followed my own way and failed the one above all and stumbled over my pride."

"Your offense is great," said the keeper. "For such pride as you have shown was First King swept from his throne and you put in his place."

"My throne is in the hands of King-Maker. I will stand aside," Shepherd King said and sank to his knees.

"For that reason he will not ask it of you. Unlike First King, you remain devoted to him and are willing to do the hard thing. King-Maker stands by his promise that your throne will be established forever.

"Yet there are consequences for your actions. Because you have humbled your heart, King-Maker will allow you to choose one of the following punishments for your failure—

"Three years of famine.

"Three months of battle.

"Three days of plague."

"The choices of King-Maker are harsher than if he were to strike me down. Once again my actions cause others to suffer. How can I choose among such painful consequences?"

The keeper knelt facing the king and put hands of comfort on his shoulders as on a penitent child. "Yes, once again you learn that the cost of listening to Shining One is seldom ours to bear alone. For leaders those consequences devastate nations. Such is the cost of King-Maker's call."

Shepherd sank down with his head to the floor. "Therefore, I will fall before King-Maker and let him do what is most fitting. It is better to rely upon his mercy than upon my own wisdom."

That very day he heard the frightening reports. People were falling ill in their homes and in the fields and even in the streets. Within a day the sickness invariably caused death. Whole families fell to the plague. A sickness that caused quick death was gripping the countryside.

"It is the angel of death," breathed Shepherd King in horror. "He walks the roads of my kingdom, devouring all he encounters."

By the afternoon of the third day thousands had been struck down. This sickness reached into nearly every corner of the Land of Promise. Shepherd King neither ate nor rested. In distress he cried out to King-Maker, offering his own death if the sickness would only subside before it reached the City of Palms.

"I did it! I am at fault!" he screamed. "Show compassion on your people. Let your hand fall against me and my family. This is too great a burden for the people and for me to bear!"

"Stop!" The voice of the one who is infinite and eternal and all-powerful echoed through creation. Even Shepherd King heard its thunder-clap of mercy. The angel of death moved no farther and the plague was over. His feet were still and he stood silent a few steps short of the City of Palms itself. A farmer and his sons were threshing wheat when they saw the glow-ing face and flaming sword of the angel. They immediately dropped their work and fled. When the king heard that the angel was striking no more, he rushed to that spot to build an altar of appreciation.

"I must buy your land to build an altar," he told the farmer over whose fields the angel had stopped.

The farmer was pale with fear.

"I will give you my land gladly, if it will stay the hand of death."

"I caused this to happen," said the king, "so I must buy the land and pay all that it is worth."

So Shepherd King bought the land and keepers of the Special Place were summoned to build an altar. Spotless, newborn lambs were sacrificed.

A warm breeze blew across the land.

"Your humility and faithfulness have saved the City of Palms," whis-pered King-Maker. The angel of death sheathed his flaming sword. As the sun settled its accounts with the day, those who survived wondered whether they had actually seen the great glowing figure cross the land.

As thousands of stars sparkled above the city that night, Shepherd King stood alone by the smoldering altar in the field he had purchased. He dreamed of a majestic temple where such sacrifices would continually be offered to the one above all. *How fitting,* he thought, *if this beautiful build-ing should stand on this very spot.*

CHAPTER 12

THE WISE KING

The aged heart of Shepherd King pounded as his hand held tight the white scroll. Carefully he unrolled the thick paper of finely woven grasses and laid it on the ground by the altar he had ordered built. He was an old man now, but today he felt like a young boy as he stood with his favorite son.

The son of the beautiful woman on the roof.

The son of a shepherd boy.

The son who was known as Peaceful One.

Together they studied the detailed drawings.

"This will be a sanctuary such as has never before been built to either Shining One or King-Maker. And this high field where the angel of death sheathed his sword—what a place to build a magnificent structure."

"When will you start to build it?" asked the son as he bent low to examine the dimensions. He glanced around, trying to imagine how such a grand building would look against the landscape. His father was silent for a moment.

"What if I did not?

"What if I could not?

"And what if you were king in my place?"

"Then, Father, I fear I might neglect the rest of the kingdom for the joy of seeing this wonder rise before King-Maker's eyes. How this place might stir all the people's hearts."

"I thought you would answer so. That is why I show these to you and speak plainly that I have asked King-Maker for permission to build this place. But he showed me the blood that will always be on my hands. He refused my request."

"Will this place then ever be built?"

"This great mission will fall to the king who comes after me. I can see this building here with the eyes of my heart. The next king will see the sun sparkle on its gold and hear footsteps echo in its halls. He will see the Ark of Mystery carried into its inner chamber."

The son looked hard at his father. "That son will be most blessed," he said. The unasked question hovered between the two men. Shepherd stooped to pick up the scrolls and roll them, tying them with a thong of leather. He handed the designs to his son.

"Keep these well, future king, until the day in which your workmen commence this great undertaking."

Thus did Peaceful One learn that his father intended that he would someday be king, though he was one of several sons, and by no means the eldest.

Shepherd King could not build the Special Place, but he could see its preparations.

Blocks of stone were quarried.

Iron nails were smelted.

Gold and silver and copper were collected.

Shepherd King gave all he owned to purchase materials for this house. When all was properly prepared he again took the future king to the site of his magnificent dream.

"When the time has come, build with love and care and devotion. And remember how I danced before the Ark of Mystery when you bring it to its new dwelling and invite King-Maker to make it his throne."

"I will do all that you say," said his son and the two embraced.

He had all he wanted, except the kingdom. But the younger brother of Rebel, the oldest living son of Shepherd, had high hopes as he walked the walls of the city. "Tomorrow I shall be king," he shouted.

Shining One smiled.

Early the next morning Rebel's brother joined the elders of the land near the City of Palms at a place called Serpent's Rock. With a commanding voice he stood before the crowd. "I have not come to divide the kingdom as did my brother. Rather it is my father's age and weakness that threatens us all. He seems unwilling to follow the path of kings and step aside for his eldest son, though his mighty days are over and the crown is too heavy for him to keep his head high. Will you accept me as your king?"

The people bowed low and cried out, "Long live the new king!"

Messengers loyal to Shepherd King raced back to the palace and told the queen. Many years had passed since the king had killed her husband and taken her as his bride. Long had she lived with the pain caused by those days. She had given up much, but she would have what had been promised.

The queen knelt by the king's bed and caressed his head as he drifted to wakefulness. He saw her, and a sparkle returned to his eyes.

"Who do you say shall be the next king?" she asked gently.

"I have but one son who will be an able ruler, who will follow the ways of King-Maker. Only one can I trust to build a great sanctuary to King-Maker. That is our own peaceful son."

"I believe your decision is right, but Rebel's brother, your eldest son, wants to take the decision from you. At Serpent's Rock he has this day declared himself king. The eyes of the kingdom are looking to you. Act quickly and decisively and fairly or all will be lost. The eldest will have the throne, and he will quickly take my life and that of our son."

Shepherd shook with anger. He raised his wrinkled hand and was helped to sit up in his bed. With a firmer voice than any had heard for months he called his royal council. The most loyal of his kingdom quickly gathered about him.

"I am no longer able to govern, but I demand the right to choose my successor. Do any deny that right?"

"Master, the brother of Rebel. . ."

"Yes, the brother of Rebel. He will not judge wisely or ably or well, and I decline to give the crown to my eldest when another is much worthier."

"If that is so we will have to act very quickly, or there will be war."

The king leaned forward with intense emotion. "Then we will act now. I declare that my reign is ended. My final command is that Peaceful One be invested and anointed and crowned this very hour."

He turned to the head keeper of the Special Place: "Will you pour King-Maker's oil on Peaceful One?"

"With a glad heart," said the keeper.

"And will all of you confidently place the crown on his head?"

"With glad hearts," they agreed.

He leaned back, his energy nearly spent. "And will you advise my son and stand by him against all who threaten his kingdom?"

"We shall!" came the unison cry.

"Then let it be done." The great voice had become a whisper, and the men hurried from the chamber to complete the most important tasks of their lives.

Golden oil dripped down the face of Peaceful One.

A sparkling crown was fitted to his head.

He was led through the City of Palms.

Rams' horns were blown and runners spread the news quickly. Music and cheers and singing echoed through the hills, until the sounds of celebrating reached the ears of Rebel's brother.

"This is wonderful. They have heard of my reign already."

"It is not for you," said an advisor. "This day your father has declared Peaceful One to be king. He has ridden the king's donkey through the streets and received the king's crown and scepter. The People of the Kingdom have heard Shepherd's wish and have pledged their hearts. If we challenge the son now we will surely stand alone, and we will certainly die."

Rebel's brother grew pale and fear filled his eyes.

"I have failed," he said with quavering voice. "Let us go and make peace with the king while we are able."

Most of his followers were already fleeing. The man who moments before was hailed as king was now rejected as traitor. In terror he fled to the Special Place and clung to the altar.

"Spare my life," he pleaded when the king had come.

"If your heart is good, I shall protect you with my life," the king said. "If your heart is evil, no one will save you."

The frightened one bowed before his brother, then returned quietly to his home. With his father's advice, the new king ruled all the land in peace.

The people were content.

The land prospered.

Peaceful King looked to the one beyond the sky.

And so did Shepherd. His body was weak and his breath short and his vision clouded. Yet he was filled with excitement. He called Peaceful One to his side.

"My heart is still that of a young shepherd, ready to go off alone into the hills with King-Maker or lift my sword to fight for him a great battle. But my heart is trapped in this prison of flesh. Soon King-Maker will open this prison door and I will run with him once more.

"So my concern is for you, my son. Listen to King-Maker and follow his ways. Draw near to him and he will draw near to you. If you are in need, go to the highlands and look beyond the sky."

The young king held his father's cold hand.

"I shall do as you say," he said softly.

With the sun touching the western horizon, Shepherd King smiled and closed his eyes and squeezed the hand of his son once more. Then he stood at the side of the one who is above all, overcome by joy and peace and love. While the City of Palms mourned, Shepherd once more picked up his harp and sang for the king—the real king.

The people bowed low and cried out, "Long live the new king!"

The king vowed not to forgot the words of his father. He rose before the sun to walk with the one who holds stars in his hands. He longed to show his devotion to the one above all, so he asked the keepers of the Special Place to make one thousand sacrifices of appreciation.

One night the king closed his tired eyes, but his vision did not dim with sleep. Before him stood a mighty angel with glowing face and tireless wings and a dreadful two-edged sword. The voice was gentle.

"You have done well in beginning your kingdom. Now choose what kind of kingdom you wish, and King-Maker shall supply all you desire with an open hand."

"I owe all I am and have to the giver of good gifts," said the king. "I do have a great need. The decisions and judgments before me are great. I fear that my intellect is too small and my judgment inadequate to the task of bringing justice to my people. Please give me a wise heart and a discerning mind, so I might know the difference between

"right and wrong,

"truth and foolishness,

"good and best."

The great angel's shining face became as brilliant as the sun, warming the humble heart.

"You have spoken very well, and I delight to grant your request. Hereafter all the Blue Planet will know you as Wise King."

The king bowed low in grateful adoration. But the angel reached down and lifted his head.

"So selfless has been your request that I shall also bless you with good things beyond your dreams.

"Your kingdom will be known for its peace.

"Your wealth will increase.

"Your name will be honored throughout the Blue Planet."

The king opened his mouth to speak, but the light was gone. A distant flutter of wings awoke the dreamer.

He wondered at what he had heard. His request was real, but was the answer? Or was it wishful imaginings? The answer came as Wise King considered all the matters brought to him. He looked upon the world and understood things hidden from others. His judgments became known for subtlety and justice and grace. Stories of his wisdom and insight and understanding spread. Large crowds gathered wherever he went, for the people longed to hear him speak so deeply and eloquently about the struggles and virtues of life.

"I am above all others most blessed," the king said gladly as he banqueted on fine foods with the princesses of other lands who had been given to be his wives by kings and governors who desired the great Wise King's favor. He thought much about all the things that gave him satisfaction.

But he began thinking less about the ways of King-Maker. And slowly, ever so quietly and gradually, the Wise King became a very intelligent fool.

SOME ERECT LIVES THAT LAST FOR TODAY
AND SOME FOR TOMORROW
AND SOME FOR FOREVER.
THE DIFFERENCE IS IN THE FOUNDATION.

CHAPTER 13

THE BUILDER AND THE HOUSE

The king unrolled the large, white scroll's thick paper. He stood back proudly as his companion wiped his shaking hands and bent low over the plans. He was very nervous, for the Chief Builder knew his life had been focused upon this moment. The builder had been little more than a boy when he had helped lay stone and boards for the palace of Shepherd King. He had watched closely and his creative eye and steady hand had come to the notice of Shepherd.

Few in the nation knew the craftsmanship needed to do great feats of construction. Indeed, few anywhere outside the Land of the Pyramids had such knowledge. So the promising young man had been sent to learn among the craftsmen of the Delta. Years later he returned to direct Shepherd King's expansion of the City of Palms and the raising of strong fortress outposts. Other promising youths had learned at his side, so that Shepherd developed one of the world's finest teams of builders to fulfill one of the world's greatest dreams—construction of a grand Special Place to King-Maker.

The Chief Builder had superintended collection of materials and overseen the quarrying of foundation stones. But until this moment he had not been allowed to see the plans for the building and its altars. All through the night he had walked with King-Maker, asking for strength and wisdom to face the challenges ahead. He stood silent now, hardly able to breathe as he inspected the plan.

"I have beheld plans for magnificent palaces and even more magnificent tombs," he murmured, without looking up from the scroll. "But never has there been such a work as this. Even on paper it breathes the fire of the altar. I am unworthy to stand before the depiction. Will these hands be able to touch the very walls enclosing the Ark of Mystery, the throne of King-Maker?"

The king nodded his understanding. "I felt less awe on the day I was anointed king than I did the first time my father unrolled this scroll. That you know your unworthiness is the sign that you are the very man chosen by the one who holds stars in his hands to turn these lines into mortar and wood and gold."

"Where. . .did such ideas come from?"

"You have read in the words of General that Promise-Keeper gave a plan for the sanctuary tent in the desert. This plan is much the same, expanded upon by my father and the keepers of the Special Place and artisans with special abilities for the work. The true designer is King-Maker."

"Then I am looking into the very heart of King-Maker, just as when I stand in the great storm or walk the rugged highlands or look beyond the star-strewn night. The design is most magnificent because it is so simple, without the ostentation or the vain secrets of the Delta pyramids, which are made to be delved only by the dead. Designers in the Delta are sometimes sacrificed to Shining One, so they will not be able to tell the hidden mysteries of the tombs. Workmen who lay the passages die in them.

"I would gladly give my life to protect the secrets of this place, yet there are none. It is a place of openness, a place for the living instead of the dead. I see that King-Maker longs to share himself with us."

"Then let us go to the keepers of the Special Place so that you may be anointed with oil. You see the hand of King-Maker. Surely you are the chosen instrument. I would rather be blessed with your understanding than with the power of many kings."

Deep into the mountain's rocky soil the workmen dug and chiseled, until they reached the bedrock at the soul of the mountain itself. Then they chiseled farther as the Chief Builder and his assistants used strange instruments to measure and level the base.

Crops were planted and tended and harvested. So much time passed, that people began to wonder if they would ever see the promised house of the one beyond the sky.

Then one day, when the colors of spring once more splashed the hillsides, the first stones were slowly moved up the mountain and down specially constructed slopes to the foundation's base. The stones seemed immovably huge. Yet the very will of the Chief Builder seemed to urge them to their resting places. As the great stones were fitted together they were backfilled with a stable mixture of sand and other soils. After one run of foundation stones came another and another and another. The stonework reached the surface of the ground, and more ramps were necessary to construct upward instead of downward. At last the walls themselves were rising.

Beams of cedar supported the roof.

Shaped stonework spread a design across the floor.

Gates swung open on iron sockets.

Interior walls smelled of a fresh-cut forest. The finest cedar boards were cut to fit one another, tongue into groove, upon the walls. Master artisans chiseled into the wood the intricate symbols of the ancient garden—the first home of Man and Woman. They carved elegant reliefs of palm trees and wild fruit, blooming flowers and hovering angels. Refined gold was pounded into thin sheets that could be shaped around the details of each carving. The walls blazed like the sun even when they reflected the night's torchlight. The gold-smiths did not stop their work when every wall glowed. They covered ceilings and floors and each corner. Now the rooms were so brilliant that even work-men who saw them each day gasped in amazement at their loveliness.

For a week of summers, thousands of builders came and labored and went home, until most families in the kingdom had shared in the shaping of the most majestic of all structures. Its wonders and artistry were discussed in every village by men who now regarded themselves as masters in masonry and woodcraft and metalwork.

The outer porch was a masterpiece in itself. Two bronze pillars invited the first glimmers from the eyes of each new dawn. Massive gold-plated doors opened to the main hall where golden lampstands flamed against amber walls. Their light seemed to set the temple on fire. Thick linen curtains of blue and purple and scarlet hung from golden rings, so that none could peek into the inner chamber. Once a year the chief keeper would push past those curtains to face the two large, golden angels with wings outstretched that guarded the ark from any who would treat King-Maker lightly.

Finally came the day when the king and nobles were called to gather before the nearly completed sanctuary. The Chief Builder unrolled the large scroll and displayed the great plans once more. Then he walked with the guests, explaining how each shimmering detail had been executed. All walked in complete silence. The king himself said not a word until their visit ended.

"If only my father could see what his dreaming has brought into being," said the king.

"I too wish that," said the Chief Builder. "But don't you suppose that this place is a poor reflection of the sanctuary in which he now stands?"

On the following day the people were invited to come and see and wonder. Fathers showed their sons what their own hands had done. Mothers held their daughters and wept at the beauty. Everyone bowed their heads in awe.

And on the third day the doors of the Special Place stood closed as a sea of people gathered on the sides of the mountain. Rams' horns blew and slowly the sacred furniture was carried up the hillside in grand procession by keepers of the sanctuary. Few infants even cried in the hot sun, so overwhelming was the scene unfolding before them. All bowed low as the Ark of Mystery was slowly borne to its new resting place.

Then when everything had been placed, the keepers spread throughout the crowd, repeating the prayers said on the great dais before the gates. Finally the king stood before the people with his hands raised to the sky.

"Hear my plea," he cried to King-Maker, "and forgive us our wanderings. . .

"Restore us to the center of your heart.

"Teach us the good ways to walk.

"Protect us from the deceptions of Shining One.

"Let us welcome you to your house where you may sit and stand and dwell among us forever.

"We know that you do not need a house," he shouted to the one beyond the sky. "But we need this place to remind us that you are always close and always care.

"Smell the pleasing fragrance of our sacrifices.

"Listen when we come to say we're sorry.

"Act in love when we bring our hurts and needs."

Suddenly none of the crowd were paying attention to these words, for the wind suddenly rose and a great cloud that seemed ablaze with light swept in from the horizon. The people stepped back in awe of the glory and power of the wind. The cloud moved through the golden doors and into the Special Place. With a flash of burning light the building glowed with a white-hot phosphorescence that forced the people to cover their eyes.

"The creator of all has heard our words. He has entered his house," proclaimed the king.

The people cried and cheered and fell on their faces.

Thousands of sacrifices were brought to be burned on the new altar before the sanctuary. The commitment was so immense that it took the entire day to finish all that had been brought.

As the sun set and darkness filled the sky, the sanctuary still glowed with a golden radiance. The people marveled at its beauty. Only slowly, hesitantly, did they turn from the courts and begin their journeys home.

The king remained standing before the Special Place in silence and solitude. He stood still and waited. The moon moved across a star-strewn sky.

"Why have you not gone with the rest?" asked the voice on the wind.

"I wait for one who gave me a wise heart."

"I am here," said the wind, "and I have heard your plea. You kept your promise to your father and the sanctuary is as majestic as he had hoped. I shall sit and stand and dwell among my people forever—long after these stones have been destroyed by time and invading armies."

"What words do you have for me?" asked the king.

"If you walk with me humbly and faithfully as your father did, all will be well. But if your heart turns away, ignoring my words and following the ways of Shining One, then your kingdom shall fall and the Special Place shall be destroyed and the people shall be scattered."

"I shall never turn away," said the king.

The wind was silent and a chill cut through the king's clothes until he shivered. A snake slithered across the courtyard with a sinister smile as the king turned toward the palace and thought of sleep.

MANY PATHS LEAD
TOWARD THE LIE,
BUT ONLY ONE
CAN LEAD TO TRUTH.

CHAPTER 14

THE WISE FOOL

Through all the summers of Wise King's rule, the people saw peace and prosperity and prestige beyond their imagining. The king built a palace even greater than that of his father and a hall of justice with a massive ivory throne overlaid with pure gold. He expanded the walls of the City of Palms and fortified strategic points to protect the land. He loved horses, so he put aside the donkeys that had been the symbol of kingship and purchased fine stallions from the desert peoples. He bred some of the finest animals on the Blue Planet and built great stables to keep them.

Knowing that his seacoast was a great asset for trade, Wise King had merchant ships built to sail toward faraway ports. He traded olive oil and wheat and even precious metals for ivory and spice and perfume. He discovered that the world's finest purple cloth was dyed with a clam that lived in his waters. Soon the Land of Promise was selling dye and the richest purple cloth that anyone on the Blue Planet had ever seen.

Where the ships went, word spread that the young kingdom was becoming great under the care of a leader with fame and fortune and wisdom. Other rulers did not overlook the amount of trade these people were doing and they wanted to share in this prosperity. Seeking alliances, they came to visit him and to seek his counsel. They offered their most beautiful daughters as princesses for the king to marry.

With each glorious gift, Wise King pointed beyond the sky and said, "I accept this in the name of the one who is eternal and infinite and all-powerful." So the name of King-Maker also spread.

Shining One hissed and spat and plotted. He was angry, but he had laid subtle traps. He knew well that each blessing in the life of Wise King was accompanied by a danger. Even the king's very understanding could be used to lure his mind away from the source of wisdom. And he saw that from the beginning, Wise King had not noticed the subtle compromises he was making in his rule.

He demanded workmen for lavish, unimportant projects.

He collected horses, ignoring King-Maker's rule not to do so.

He loved beautiful women and made many of them his own.

With the added wealth of the people, Shining One saw the great possibilities for luring the people to his side. Shining One quietly encouraged the king in his compromises, and by the time he was an old man his heart was wrapped up in women and wealth and horses. No longer did he spend long hours standing near the altars of the sanctuary. Only on special occasions did he even think of the sanctuary at all. And he flattered himself that even as an old man he could be a vigorous husband and lover and provider to the hundreds of women he had gathered under his care.

Among the women were the graceful daughter of the Delta King and sun-kissed princesses of the People of the Plains and fair maidens from beyond the Mountains of the Dawn. He could be with any of a thousand women, who were all beautiful and all willful and all followers of Shining One.

"I long for the valleys and lowlands of the Delta," said the princess from the Land of the Pyramids.

"I will send a guard to go with you on a visit to your people if you wish."

"You are such a good and thoughtful husband. What would make me most happy would be a bit of soil from my land on which a shrine to the sun might be built. I know you do not follow that way, but it would mean much to me."

A few summers later she was back at his side.

"Several of us who honor the sun have been gathering at the shrine you built for me. Some have asked if you might come join us for our special holy day tomorrow."

"No, that would not be right, for you know that I trust only in King-Maker."

"And that is as it should be for the strong and wise and benevolent king of all the people. You need not turn from what you think right. You need only honor and respect those who follow other ways. Toss a pinch of incense into the flame. What could that hurt?"

"It does not seem right."

"But they would look upon me at your side. Oh, it would mean so much to me. And I have always been so happy in your love. If that is changing. . ."

So the king went, and his wife was indeed most happy. But all the other women from all the other nations were most unhappy.

So he built temples for them,
and he joined them at their shrines
and bowed before statues of the snake.

He tried to speak against the serpent, and sometimes he forced them to come to the Special Place to honor King-Maker with him. But this hurt them and caused a certain coldness when they were together. Without exception, the women of his harem prevailed. Wise King found himself on a continual tour of temples and altars and statues to Shining One.

As he stood before one of these altars, the wind blew hard and cold and angry.

"I do not know this place. What are you doing in it?"

"I love you and will always look to you. I only want to please my wives."

"You no longer know how it is to please me." The wind cut through his clothing as the words slashed at his pretense. "You have left my path and followed the ways of another. You have broken the promise of your kingship."

"It is so hard to please everyone," said the king with his head low.

"Then you have made your decisions of whom to please. You have split your loyalties in front of all the People of Promise. You have brought shame upon me and disaster upon my people. So I will split your kingdom in front of all the Blue Planet. The northern part will be torn from the hands of your sons. Many will die and never know to turn to me."

Wise King buried his face in his hands and wept at his foolishness.

Several cycles of the moon later, a young man with strong arms and great abilities walked alone on an isolated portion of road not far from the City of Palms. He had been born in the north, near the Place of the Portal, and his father had died when he was a small child. When the king needed workers, the young man went to the City of Palms. His hard work and leadership had caught the eye of the king and he had risen to prominence as an elder in his tribe.

"Hail, king!"

The source of the voice was behind him. He turned and recognized the speaker as a spokesperson for King-Maker, a great keeper of the Special Place.

"Why do you give me such a strange greeting? I am only a servant of the king and the people. I'm not even one of the king's sons, and he has plenty of those."

"I am only giving the words of the one above all. He sent me to seek you and told me where to find you on this road."

"Why do you come to me?" asked the young man with suspicion. He had never been particularly interested in following King-Maker.

"Wise King has not walked humbly and faithfully before King-Maker as did his father. The women he married have turned his heart toward Shining One. Therefore King-Maker will divide his kingdom, giving you the tribes of the north to rule. If you hear his words and walk his ways and keep his commands, then he will pass this rule from father to child for many generations."

The young man told his friends. His friends went among the northern cities and spoke well of him. Many still remembered that First King had been from among them and they were not altogether pleased with the rule of Shepherd's son.

Wise King was furious when he learned that the young man he had helped was about to declare himself ruler of the north. How could anyone so brazenly threaten the peace and prosperity and prestige of his kingdom?

"Find this man," he ordered. "Take his life before he stirs the people against me."

The young man was in the City of Palms and would soon have lost his life had not his friends inside the palace warned him to flee. With only the clothes he wore and a bag of bread, he slipped from the city. The guards heard of his escape and pursued, but he hid in the hills and slept in caves. When the way was clear he fled south to the Land of the Delta. There he lived in silence and waited for the death of Wise King.

As the king's breath grew short and his eyes dim, he thought back on his life. He reflected on the words of his father:

"Forgive my wanderings," he said to the one above all.

"Restore me to the center of your heart.

"Welcome me to your house where I may sit with you forever."

Soon his sons gathered and mourners prepared to mourn. The king sat up in his bed to speak:

"I have looked for happiness and satisfaction in so many ways:

"Wisdom.

"Pleasure.

"Fame and fortune.

"I have come to realize that it is all a chase after nothing. It all is worthless. Only one thing has worth—to walk with King-Maker and follow his ways.

"Before the silver cord is cut

"and the golden bow broken

"and dust becomes dust once more

"remember the one beyond the sky who hold stars in his hands and makes all things beautiful in their time. In each heart he plants a longing for eternity. He alone is true and good and pure."

Those around his bed leaned close and listened. The king worked to see those all around, but his eyes no longer focused. He cleared his throat and breathed a deep, rattling breath. As he spoke his voice was soft and calm and contented:

"There are many paths on the landscape of eternity, but only one has meaning. He who turns from it is a fool. I was a fool. Don't follow my way, but walk that path with the ruler of all, for light is better than darkness."

A smile crossed his lips as he heard the familiar music of Shepherd. He looked up and took the hand of his father and left the Blue Planet behind. As the sun set on the magnificent sanctuary and the royal palace, father and son walked with King-Maker together, never again to turn away.

EPILOGUE

The man with the long, gray beard stood by the dying embers, as the night chill stole into the circle. He looked to the dark sky, with its thousand glistening diamonds.

"Light is certainly better than darkness," he murmured.

The men shook their heads in agreement. The women wearily wrapped their arms around sleepy children or prodded them in the direction of home.

But a girl who had known nine summers and dearly loved to ask questions wandered from her mother and came to the old man's side.

"Grandfather," she said as her soft fingers clutched his large, calloused hand. "Was Wise King really the smartest man on the Blue Planet?"

"King-Maker gave him much wisdom and knowledge and insight."

"Then why didn't he follow King-Maker? That seems a lot wiser than what he did."

"You are right, little one. He did not use his wisdom when he most needed it. Even the wisest can be distracted or deceived," the storyteller said sadly.

"But not if you walk with King-Maker in the highlands, right?"

"Walk with him wherever you are, and you won't be deceived."

Her mother was calling impatiently, but the child was still thinking through this.

She tapped her small chest. "It is better to have a smart heart from walking with the one beyond the sky than a smart head from learning."

The old man smiled.

"It is best to have the smart heart from holding King-Maker close—and the smart head from learning as well."

PART 2
THE HOPE-GIVER

TABLE OF CONTENTS
The Hope-Giver

PROLOGUE

Fire flickered to light the face of the man with a hundred wrinkles. The circle of people watched the storyteller as he asked two young men to move a heavy wooden table out of the darkness. At his command others set torches near the table, close enough to cast light, but not so close as to send sparks upon its smooth and shiny top.

"I have something to show you," said the old man as he unfolded an old piece of heavy parchment. It was thick and yellowed with age. When he had spread it across the table he let the people come up, a few at a time, so their shadows would not obscure the view. There were gasps of "Ooh!" and "Aah!" It was a beautiful map, carefully etched with a delicate pen and artfully highlighted with exotic pigments.

"Behold the New Land. This is the part of the Blue Planet set aside for the people of Promise-Keeper and Land-Giver and King-Maker." He held it up so all could see.

"Here is the Great Sea and the Salty Sea. Here is the Winding River and the Western River and the Mountains of the Dawn."

Now the storyteller folded the map once, down the middle. He looked closely at the people.

"After the passing of Wise King, brother turned against brother and tore the kingdom in two."

With a violent movement the precious parchment ripped along the fold. It seemed the paper itself screamed, and all the people gasped. There were shouts of "No!" and "Don't!"

The old man held the pieces out in his two hands and cried. "This is what happens to the people who forget the one above all! They are torn apart." He held one piece up to the torch on his left. People cried out again as the paper caught fire. He held the bottom half to the top. Now they both flamed.

The girl who had known nine summers ran to her grandfather.

"The beauty is all gone."

"Yes, child, that happens when we take our eyes off King-Maker."

"Did he leave them forever?"

"He did not leave them at all. But he did give them new names to know him by. To the Southern Kingdom he was Hope-Giver."

"Did they need hope?" the little girl asked.

"Watch," he told her with a smile. She stepped back, and he reached into a fold of his robe and pulled something out. He unfolded it. Everyone stood and came close, laughing with wondrous relief that the priceless map had not been torn and burned after all.

"Oh, my little one," the old man said, looking at the girl. "We all must have hope."

And so he began.

> A PEOPLE TORN IN TWO
> SACRIFICE STRENGTH
> AND POTENTIAL.

CHAPTER 1

THE DIVIDED PEOPLE

He held his father's hand as Wise King let go of the Blue Planet. He held tightly to the limp fingers and listened to the final words and vowed he would be a better king than his father.

Kings do not weep, and the Chosen Son wiped away the speck of water threatening his vision. He stood strong before those who mourned.

"A great man has left us. Now we must crown our next king."

Elders of the tribes journeyed to the City of Oaks. The people gathered around the son Wise King had chosen.

A delegation of elders representing the northern tribes asked to meet privately with the prince.

"Your father accomplished a great many things," said the spokesman. "His was a time of peace and prosperity and prestige. He built a majestic sanctuary and an impressive palace. He raised walls and fortresses. Even stables.

"But he did not do it alone. Your father placed heavy burdens on the people; he made life difficult. Many of the king's projects were not worth the pain they caused. We will do all that we can to support your kingdom. We simply ask that you lighten our load."

The prince had thought of these things. He knew the request was reasonable. But it did not seem right when someone else said it. These elders were deciding whether to crown him. The very idea! He was about to lead a kingdom that his father had made great. Was he now to sit in his father's palace and listen to the people's woes? Then what would he be remembered for?

He said none of this. Neither did he agree to their request.

"Give me time to consider," he said. "Then I will give you my answer."

Many days' journey south, messengers from the northern tribes had reached the young man who had escaped to the Land of the Delta.

"Wise King has passed. Chosen Son will soon be anointed and crowned. But he lacks heart and wisdom and discretion. Will you come? Will you come quickly?"

A fine stallion was purchased. With food and water and sword the young man galloped away, leaving far behind the messengers on their camels.

As fast as he could travel through the desert, watching only for raiders, he sped to the City of Oaks. Courage and pride and his memory of what the keeper had said to him drove the young man on.

As the traveler thought these things, the son of Wise King was meeting with his father's counselors about the entreaty of the northern peoples.

"The people loved your father. If they had not they would not have served him as they did. But his rule was harsh. This request is reasonable. After all, you need their support," said the advisors.

"So listen to the people.

"Show compassion.

"Lighten their load."

He dismissed these counselors with his thanks and called together his closest friends.

"Each king has need of sound minds," he told them, "and the minds of my father's counselors are full of practicality and caution and treason. So I turn to you."

The young men knew their friend and what he liked to hear.

"It is good that you have come to us, or your kingdom would be over before it begins. These men do not want your strong rule. They think they can run over you. Tell them you are firmly in command and will build a kingdom more glorious than that of anyone before you. If your father gave them a heavy load, you will break their backs until they submit to your majesty."

The son smiled, "Your advice is strong. That is what I shall do."

On the third day he stood before the elders. "You are soft!" he yelled. "You dream of lazy, carefree afternoons. I shall not tolerate such wasteful ways, so I shall double and triple your loads. With sweat and strain we shall build a kingdom as great as any on the Blue Planet."

"But we cannot do as much as we have done, let alone double it," pleaded the people.

"You shall do as I command."

The people turned slowly away, uncertain and sorrowful and angry.

"It is as we expected," said one.

"It is worse," said another.

The young man ignored the crowd and took his crown. *He would deal with those who opposed him quickly,* he fumed. He called the elders into his presence once more.

The king was just taking his place on a fine throne built for the occasion when the crowd parted and a man not many years older than himself strolled confidently through. A great sword was strapped to his back. The guards wanted to grab this potential threat, but the king dismissed their concerns with a haughty wave of the hand.

"Who are you? Why have you come before me armed for war?" he demanded.

The crowd grew deathly still, straining to hear the reply.

"I am the next king of the Land of Promise. I come to see why an unworthy pretender is detaining my elders from their work."

Everybody gasped, at the arrogance—and audacity.

The young king was afraid of this leader that his father had tried to kill. He managed a sneer.

"I claim my throne by the choice of my father, the supreme ruler of this land. May I ask what great council has given you my scepter?"

"No council. I was chosen by the one above all, who holds stars in his hands. Your father bowed to King-Maker. But now King-Maker finds you unworthy and has given your throne to another. He has given it to me," said the challenger with brazen confidence. "King-Maker has given me the tribes of the North, and I will take the South as well."

The crowd roared with both celebration and protest.

"If the Chosen Son will not lighten our loads, let us crown Challenger," cried the northern tribes.

"Chosen Son has acted foolishly, but he will grow. Remember his grandfather. Remember his father," said one from the tribe of the royal family. "We have already anointed and crowned him."

"We have not given our consent to it," shouted a northerner.

"I am next in Shepherd's line," declared the king to the people. "I am king, with or without your assent. I demand your submission."

The nervous guards moved forward to seize the man with the big sword and treasonous words. But they hesitated when the northern elders formed a wall about him.

"We refuse to follow one who will not hear our suffering," said the man who had spoken for the North in the meeting with the king. "Order your armed men to strike us down. But then see what becomes of your kingdom." The delegation turned and left the plaza. The Challenger mounted a fine white stallion and slowly led the way, as though he were leading them toward a noble battle. The guards looked to the king, who stood with only the small band of southern elders.

"Will you be our new king?" the Challenger was asked as the procession made its way north.

Before he could answer, a spokesman from the South ran to catch up. "Please, brothers, we have come so far together. Much blood has been poured onto this soil on behalf of the kingdom of Shepherd. You cannot reject his grandson and see it all split apart."

"Much of that blood was the blood of our fathers. They did not give their lives so that we might be slaves as in the Land of the Delta. The decision belongs to your new king. Will he meet our demands?"

"Can he meet them now without being shamed?" asked the spokesman. "Of course not. Be patient."

"No longer! We declare that the kingdom is divided, and we will go our way with the Challenger as our king."

"If you refuse to submit, the army will crush you."

"Threaten if you wish. We will not submit."

Soon two young kings faced each other across the mountains and valleys of the New Land. The Challenger was crowned with the blowing of many rams' horns, among thousands of his northern countrymen. Dancing and singing and feasting lasted long into a star-studded night.

The king of the South mustered every warrior within his kingdom against the North. But the elders had been correct: He had a far smaller army than he had supposed.

Warriors sharpened their swords
and prepared their arrows
and strengthened their shields.

When all was ready, both armies gathered and waited to be led into battle by their kings.

The Southern King was preparing to stand before his troops and speak when a trusted keeper of the Special Place spoke sternly to him: "Do not send your soldiers against their brothers."

"I will fight for my kingdom."

"Your father turned from King-Maker and his kingdom has been divided. King-Maker has given the northern tribes to Challenger. He will not be given the Southern Kingdom, for King-Maker will honor his promise that your family will always have a throne. But if you go to war against your brothers, King-Maker will not go with you."

The words touched the young king, who remembered the errors of his father. Already his own foolishness had cost much.

"If King-Maker is not with us, we will not fight," said the king. He went out to his warriors and said: "There will be no war. Go home to your wives and children and fields. We may have to gather against our brothers later, but they must start the fight. We will begin anew and rebuild the kingdom that King-Maker has given to us."

The men gladly obeyed. The fields of the New Land saw no blood.

The wind blew gentle and the Southern King let it kiss his sorrowing face. He looked upward and asked, "Challenger will come. How will I protect your kingdom?"

"Listen to my words and walk in my ways. I shall share with you a new name by which you and your children and your children's children may look to me."

"Our people have known you by many names: Garden-Maker and Promise-Keeper, Bondage-Breaker and Land-Giver and People-Builder. You have blessed my family as King-Maker. Your names have told us much about who you are. I would be honored to see deeper into the heart of the one beyond the sky."

"Yes, I am Garden-Maker and Promise-Keeper and Bondage-Breaker. I have served my people as Land-Giver and People-Builder and King-Maker," whispered the wind, "but my people now need me as Hope-Giver, for that is what I always am. All who look to me shall have hope."

For three summers the king of the south walked with Hope-Giver as his grandfather did. He listened to the wind and looked beyond the sky and sacrificed spotless, newborn lambs to the one above all.

The king of the North was a practical man who followed King-Maker as it served his ends. The Special Place of the one beyond the sky was in the heart of the city of his enemy; the old ways of sacrifice and honor definitely would have to change.

"Until we unite the kingdom we must provide for our people, so that they can worship him who holds the stars in his hands," he told his advisors. "I propose building temporary altars, and we will choose good men to be keepers of our sanctuaries. King-Maker surely would have it no other way."

But they did not honor King-Maker; they honored Shining One. The people did not learn the name of Hope-Giver. In the South, life was not so harsh under the young king.

He learned to listen
and show compassion
and lighten the load of his people.

But most important he learned to look beyond the sky and teach his people to walk with the one who gives hope.

If only he had always followed that path.

> TO TRUST IN WHAT IS UNTRUSTWORTHY
> IS ULIMATELY TO SUFFER LOSS.

CHAPTER 2

THE WARRIOR KING

His kingdom had been cut in two by his father's pride. The Southern King wept at his own foolishness and cried for help from Hope-Giver. It was good that the richest parts of the New Land, as well as the strongest cities, were in his realm. But his wealth gave the Southern King more reason for envy. He wanted *all* the nation that Wise King had ruled. The Southern Kingdom also looked appealing to other nations, a succulent morsel to consume.

Fortunately the Southern King had learned to lead instead of demand. He humbly asked for help, and together his people turned to the task of fortifying their cities.

Workmen built stone garrisons.

Supplies of grain and wine were gathered.

The king found swords and shields and spears.

Veteran commanders trained the warriors until they could stand against any army.

Feeling more secure, the king became distracted from following Hope-Giver. He did not intend to turn his back. The demands of rebuilding a nation were simply too great. Like his grandfather and his father before him he became too busy to walk the highlands each morning. Soon he no longer listened to the wind or looked beyond the sky or sacrificed spotless, newborn lambs. As summers passed he drifted toward the ways of his mother, a princess of the People of the Plains—devoted to Shining One.

When their king became interested in temples and altars and statues, so did many of the people.

In anger Hope-Giver stirred the heart of the Delta King to desire the wealth of the Southern Kingdom. An army from the Land of Pyramids burst through the valleys, swallowing whole cities with their chariots and horsemen and foot soldiers.

Walls were battered.

Fields and flocks were destroyed.

Swords and shields and spears lay broken.

Soon the enemy surrounded the City of Palms itself. Southern King was afraid of the punishment Hope-Giver might lay upon him, and he was ashamed of his faithlessness. So he made matters worse by turning to Shining One. The king cried and begged and shouted before his own serpentine shrine, yet the attack went on.

A keeper of the Special Place was heard in the market: "You have abandoned Hope-Giver. Why should he not abandon you?"

The keeper pointed to the city gate: "See what happens when Hope-Giver withdraws."

A battering ram had been pounding on the gate's timbers for days. As the keeper pointed, the great gate shivered and shuddered and shattered. Soldiers came running, but the enemy had already won the city gate. Soon they had ransacked the palace, taking the golden throne and goblets and crown.

"What can we do?" the king asked the keeper.

"You have tried the hope of Shining One. You have only Hope-Giver left. Go to him and see if he will listen, for he alone can save your city."

The invaders looking for gold and silver received unexpected help. The Southern King shattered his snake shrine and sent the precious metals to the Delta Army. Elders went throughout the city and even to the surrounding villages smashing the valuable shrines. Then elders and people and king repented in tears.

The invaders laughed as they burst through the temple doors and stole all they could find. They even stripped gold from the floor and ceiling and walls of Hope-Giver's Special Place.

Suddenly dark clouds covered the city. Thunder rolled and lightning flashed and the ground shook. Within the inner chamber, the Ark of Mystery pulsated with a yellow glow that poured terror into the invaders' hearts. A low, steady moan grew. Then the air exploded with a scorching light. The army grabbed its pillage and fled frantically from the city, back toward the Delta.

The city celebrated by gathering before the magnificent Special Place. They sacrificed thousands of spotless, newborn lambs and turned their faces to the sky. The clouds broke and the sun shared its light and a rainbow stretched across the highlands. Its vivid colors reminded them of the ancient vow that Garden-Maker had made to Builder after waters covered the Blue Planet: He was always close and would always care.

"The ways of Hope-Giver are not easy," complained the Southern King one day.

"How true," commented his amiable visitor, raising his goblet in agreement. "Hope-Giver demands much time and effort and commitment," said the one whose pinched features looked somewhat snakelike.

"Early walks with Hope-Giver are fine for children. But I have battles to fight and a kingdom to reunite," said the king, who had drunk enough to feel relaxed and fuzzy and sleepy.

"There are easier ways," said the snake. "I hold the Blue Planet in my hands. My way is easy. Follow me using any path you wish."

"But where were you when I needed you?" chided the king drunkenly.

"I wanted to see if you would be as good as your word," answered the serpent. "You tucked your tail and cringed before Hope-Giver. Let him help you."

The answer made sense, so the Southern King set about proving his loyalty.

Statues were molded.

Altars were rebuilt.

Temples were raised once more.

So Hope-Giver held back his blessing. The days of the first Southern King were filled with war, and the king knew no peace.

The king had several wives and many children, but one son was his favorite. Early this boy showed a strong will and an aggressive nature and a love of the tales of battle. Before his fifth summer his father was calling him Little Warrior.

Day after day Little Warrior placed pebbles in his own small sling and practiced hitting the ancient olive trees just outside the city walls. He puffed up his chest. "I am Shepherd!" he shouted at the trees. "Send your mightiest giant for me to slay."

During his tenth summer, the king gave his son a superbly balanced sword that was the envy of his brothers. At thirteen summers he could fight with soldiers. By seventeen his father could no longer stand against his skill and speed. Within a handful of summers he was undeniably the champion of the Southern Kingdom.

Border skirmishes between North and South grew more deadly. Each spring the Southern King gathered a large war band against his northern kinsmen. Little Warrior fought alongside his father. He proved his courage and was made a commander. The Southern King was proud. His son was a warrior fit to wear the crown.

The next spring the king struck with many men to capture the Place of the Portal—the special city near the place where Schemer had seen the massive silver staircase stretched beyond the sky. The North met them well-prepared. In the midst of a ferocious battle, the Southern King found himself separated from the protection of his guard. Enemy soldiers surrounded him and cut him down. The army of the Southern Kingdom picked up their dying king and fled from the field.

No one hesitated to declare that Little Warrior was now Warrior King. Who would dare dispute with his sword? The new king's first act was to storm into the temple of Shining One and confront its keepers.

"Where is the king's long life?

"Where is the victory?

"Where is the united kingdom?"

A quiet, reasonable voice answered as a snake glided from behind the statue itself.

"Such impatience does not become great kings," the ancient serpent yawned. "I cannot be blamed if your father did not follow the rules of battle. Did your father do anything he did not wish? Did I push him onto the enemy swords? Such are the fortunes of war—fortunes that made you king."

"Your defense is that you did nothing?" Warrior King aimed the point of his sword menacingly close to the serpent's flickering tongue.

"You might be surprised what I can do," hissed the snake angrily. "Why don't you try me?"

"Give to me what you promised my father: victory and long life. Then I will follow you."

"You may wish for anything," said the snake. "Am I not good to my servants?"

Warrior King sheathed his sword and turned his back and marched out of the temple, chuckling.

"I have shamed and tricked Shining One into giving us what we want," he said to his aide with a wry smile.

With a more serpentine grin, Shining One turned to his followers, "I do love fools who think they are as subtle as I. I will take my revenge on his insolence."

Warrior King and his brothers laid their father near the bones of Wise

King and Shepherd King. Then the following spring, Warrior King gathered his warriors. Before they marched north, a keeper of the Special Place stood before the king.

"Hope-Giver has given me a dream. I have seen a great battle. A wave of sharp swords swept down from the North and washed over the Army of the South. Your soldiers died without mercy and you, oh king, fell. You were without fear, but you fell to the judgment of Hope-Giver."

The king was not so foolish as to dismiss the dire warning.

"What can I do to lead my men to true victory?" asked the king.

"Has someone suggested that you can have true victory without the presence of Hope-Giver? You are misinformed. You can still receive pardon. But if you choose Hope-Giver, dare not turn from him again."

Warrior King sacrificed a spotless, newborn lamb to the one above all and cried to the one beyond the sky. "Forgive me for listening to the words of Shining One and walking the ways of darkness."

"Follow me," whispered the wind.

"I will follow," said Warrior King as he led his army north. The next day he faced an enemy much stronger than his army.

"Take courage," Warrior King told his men.

He climbed a small hill overlooking the enemy lines and lifted high the sword his father had given him. Then he shouted something the Northern Army had not expected:

"Shining One is a liar and thief!

"Hope-Giver is our sword and shield!

"He is our victory."

He implored the northern soldiers: "Come with us. Together let us sacrifice spotless, newborn lambs at the Special Place built by my grandfather. Let us follow only the one who is infinite and eternal and all-powerful."

While this speech went on, the king of the Northern Army was quietly but quickly using the distraction to position a small force behind Warrior King and the Southern Kingdom's army, At the blast of a ram's horn, the Northern Army rushed forward from all sides. Seeing his men panic, Warrior King cried out to Hope-Giver, "Be our victory!"

Confidence touched the heart of every southern soldier. Each looked beyond the sky. Then in perfect unison the keepers of the Special Place blew their rams' horns and the soldiers raised a battle cry that shook the hills and frightened the northern soldiers.

The ferocity and unity of the assault was awe-inspiring and terrifying. The northern attack was broken and the northern soldiers fled. The Southern Kingdom pursued relentlessly and won a handful of cities, including the Place of the Portal.

"Hope-Giver is our victory!" shouted Warrior King.

"He is our only hope," replied his army.

Yet Warrior King did not really believe that. He was certain he could use Shining One as well as Hope-Giver, playing antagonists against one another. It wasn't that Shining One had given him much reason for confidence, but Hope-Giver's way seemed so demanding.

He forgot the words of the keeper of the Special Place.

In the third spring of his reign, Warrior King again led his men north. Before leaving the City of Palms he went to the temple of Shining One to ask for victory and long life.

"Have whatever you wish," said the snake in blessing.

The king was hungry for battle and his men confident that none could stand before their might. Suddenly a ram's horn blew and a wave of foot soldiers swept upon them.

The ambush was well laid and the place well chosen. Though greatly outnumbered, Warrior King would not retreat. The fighting was fierce and the ground turned red. Still, the king pressed his men forward. All day metal struck metal and many fell. As day's light drew toward its end, three northern swordsmen managed to slash their way to the king.

They were large and strong and determined.

They pressed him with fury.

Blood flowed from his leg and shoulder.

"Give me strength," he cried out to Shining One. But there was no answer.

He felt the shock of unbelievable pain. A strong hand was thrusting a blade ever deeper into his side. *I have finally been beaten,* he thought in surprise, as his legs gave way.

Before the sun rose above the Mountains of the Dawn, soldiers slowly bore the body of their king back to the City of Palms.

Warrior King was mourned as a hero of great courage, but one who was deceived. Without Hope-Giver, he saw neither victory nor long life.

GOODNESS ALONE
WILL LOSE ITS LUSTER,
BUT GOODNESS WITH FAITH
IS A TREASURE
THAT WILL NEVER FADE.

CHAPTER 3

THE GOOD KING

I will not be as foolish as my father," promised the oldest son of Warrior King as a gold crown was set upon his head.

This young man was soon known as the Good King, for all his heart and soul and strength belonged to Hope-Giver.

As a child Good King had noticed many things. He had walked alongside his grandfather in the dawn with Hope-Giver and saw the country blessed. He also saw his grandfather fall away, more than once, each time at a cost. The boy watched his grandmother, the haughty princess of a far-off people, grow unhappy and bitter in hatred toward the People of the Promise and especially Hope-Giver. Perhaps she was why his father had begun well but fell so quickly into the snares of Shining One.

Nothing seemed so obvious to Good King than that it was better to follow Hope-Giver. At first he may have followed for selfish reasons, so that he could have good things from the one above all. But few doubted that the son of Warrior loved Hope-Giver with an inner love and a tender heart and a willing mind. He awoke before the sun and walked the highlands. He banished the voice of the ancient serpent when it enticed him and kept his ear constantly open to the whispers on the wind. The king urged the people to turn their faces away from Shining One.

He destroyed the dark temples.

He tore down the evil altars.

He shattered the serpentine statues.

Good King did all that was right and noble and pure. The people respected him above all others in the Southern Kingdom, and they followed his footsteps. Hope-Giver smiled peace and prosperity across the land. Minor skirmishes continued with the Northern Kingdom, but there was no war. It was a time of rest from fighting. A tranquillity settled upon the country such as was known in the days of Wise King.

As at all times on the Blue Planet, kings made alliances and grew strong and declined and fell. At the headwaters of the Wide River, the wondrous river that flowed through the Delta, an ancient people had become strong and made a league with the People of the Pyramids. The Headwaters People assembled a great army under an able commander, with three hundred chariots and thousands of war-ready foot soldiers. They invaded the New Land along the Great Sea and then cut across the highlands to capture the City of Palms.

Good King had distant outposts connected by good roads, so he knew quickly of the threat. His spies shadowed the invaders' every move. Before the great army neared the City of Palms he went out to meet his foe with his own army of brave fighting men. From the highlands the king looked down into the Valley of Sheep on those who wished to destroy his people.

He looked beyond the sky and cried out, "These people have only Shining One, but he is nothing to you!

"No other is so true.

"No other is so awesome.

"No other is so mighty.

"We are nothing to this vast army, and we need your help. Without your hand, many good men will die here."

So the hand of Hope-Giver shook the valley and flung fire from the sky. The enemy could not stand against such forces. Those who were not struck down left behind their weapons and fled as far as they could before collapsing.

A great wealth had been left at their base camp. There were many fine weapons and much armor. There were horses and sheep and camels. Many wagons were filled with plunder.

When soldiers and wagons returned to the City of Palms, they were welcomed as heroes. A parade wound through the city. Palm branches were waved and spread before the warriors.

The king called the people together before the Special Place. He lifted his hands, and all became quiet. "Our soldiers fought with courage, but Hope-Giver gave us victory. Without him, many of you would be wailing for your husbands and fathers and sons."

Several summers later the voice of the wind spoke to a young keeper of the temple. The keeper went to the king and told him the words of the wind: "Hope-Giver is with you. Only walk with him. But if you turn away, you will stumble and fall."

Good King thought long on these words. He yearned to be closer to Hope-Giver, and he wished his people had a deeper desire. During the years of prosperity, many had neglected the ways of the one above the sky. They had been enticed to the easier paths of Shining One.

Good King called a great gathering and stood before the people. "Today is a day to turn from deception. Some of you have built temples or altars or statues to Shining One. Together let us decide that they do not belong among us. Let us destroy them all."

The king also called stone craftsmen to the Special Place, where the great altar had been neglected, for few were bringing sacrifices. He called upon the elders and showed them the altar. Soon many were coming to the City of Palms with cattle and sheep and doves to be sacrificed. The one beyond all watched the sweet smoke rise to linger with the clouds. He heard his people promise to seek him with all their heart and soul and strength. They raised their eyes and their hands and their voices. It was a good day in the Southern Kingdom. The sun shone more bright and beautiful than anyone could remember. The king knelt before the rebuilt altar and thanked Hope-Giver for every good gift.

Yet some refused to raise their eyes. They hardened their hearts and clung to Shining One and taught others to worship the darkness. The king wept at what he saw. He decreed that those who followed the serpent must die, so the nation would not stumble and fall.

In making such a stern decree he was not thinking about the one in his own family who was the leader in following Shining One. His ancient grandmother still held great power. She was stubborn and uncompromising and full of conspiracies. She had made herself a serpentine statue and plated it with gold. Emeralds looked out from its hollow eyes. Every day she bowed before this image and encouraged others to do the same.

"There is no victory in Shining One," her grandson told her. "He is a liar and a thief."

"I don't care what you say." The wrinkled woman shook as she spoke. "The snake is my protector. I shall never forsake him."

"Please hear my words," begged the king, "and walk in the light."

Soldiers took away the wooden image.

They peeled away the gold.

They plucked out its eyes.

They burned it in the garbage heap.

"Why won't you let me worship as I wish, instead of trying to force me to walk with you? Why do you harm my sacred statue?" she cried.

"To show you that the power of Shining One is evil and worthless. It did nothing to those who pulled down the altars and killed the keepers and burned your statue. I must purify all the nation of this evil. Are you ready to seek the one above all?" demanded the king.

"I will not."

No matter what the king said, his grandmother would not bend. So the king took away her power and told her to prepare to die. He loved his grandmother, but his heart belonged to Hope-Giver. The next morning she was gone, having fled east to a land deceived by the snake and lost in darkness.

More years of peace and prosperity passed. Then the Northern King grew restless. He built a powerful army. He sent his soldiers into the land of Good King. A handful of cities fell, and the Northern King fortified them so that they could not be easily retaken. One of these towns was not far from the City of Palms, so that worry plagued the king's waking hours and nightmares marred his sleep. The Northern Army was within striking distance of his capital and their intention was clear.

"What shall we do?" Good King asked his advisors. "The Southern Kingdom is in grave danger."

One practical elder had an idea: "Take the silver and gold you plundered from the Army of the Headwaters People. Send it to the king of the City of Caravans. Tell him you will make him wealthy if he sends troops into the Northern Kingdom."

This seemed a wise act, and the king of the City of Caravans readily accepted the agreement. He attacked the Northern Kingdom, capturing the cities of the far north and the storage towns near the Stormy Sea.

Northern King quickly pulled back his forces to protect his own lands and recapture the towns near the Stormy Sea. Without adequate defenses, the towns that had been taken from Good King were easily taken back.

All was well. Now the king slept soundly, until the day a man of truth came to the palace with fire in his throat.

"Why did you rely on the might of another king? Do you not know the one who is able to make kings and break kingdoms?"

"I believe I have done well. I avoided war and did nothing to dishonor Hope-Giver. Who are you to question me?"

"Mine is the voice of Hope-Giver. He has given these words to me. When you faced the Headwaters People, you relied on the one above all. You had no choice. But when your northern brothers attacked, you relied on silver and gold. You did not seek Hope-Giver. Instead you sought your own advisors. You never looked beyond the sky."

This strong condemnation filled the king with anger.

"I have heard too much of your ramblings. Hope-Giver can come to me if he has any complaints."

The man of truth shook his head. "The eyes of Hope-Giver search throughout the Blue Planet to bless those whose hearts are fully committed to him. You have always been committed, but your wavering showed a lack of faith. This is a serious error that has cost you the blessing on your people. Now you will know war and trouble for all the rest of your life."

The king would not be spoken to so harshly. He exploded in fury.

"Bind this traitor," said the king. "Hold him with the prisoners awaiting judgment for their crimes."

So the man of truth was brutally beaten. He was thrown into a dungeon among the criminals until Good King realized his foolishness. He released the man of truth and welcomed him to his table.

"You were right," said the king. "Hope-Giver is my only hope. To look anywhere else for protection or wisdom or help is foolishness."

The times did grow dark and troubled. Good King was humbled and he walked once more with the one beyond the sky. But he was becoming old, and his walking became more painful. His morning meetings grew shorter. His body was crippled and his spirit crushed. One day as the king was overseeing a project outside the City of Palms, his body wavered and his face grimaced. He collapsed onto a large stone to catch his breath and ease his torment.

His feet had an unnatural color.

His ankles were swollen and disfigured.

His legs could no longer carry his weight.

Servants now had to carry him in his bed. Healers attended him with herbs and cures and words of wisdom, but his pain only grew worse. In desperation the king sent messengers to other kingdoms in search of healers. For three more summers the finest healers of the known world came to the City of Palms, but none could help. His feet became lame and his heart discouraged and his once joyful face filled with misery.

One day the man of truth appeared again and was brought to Good King's bedside. "Once more you have made wrong choices. With all you know, why did you not think to turn to Hope-Giver instead of relying on all these healers? Most of them are followers of Shining One, and they have done you more harm than good."

The king wept at his foolishness, but it was too late. The next evening, as the moon shone full on a clear canvas of black, he said good-bye and left the Blue Planet, freed from his years of torment to walk once more with Hope-Giver.

For over forty summers Good King had ruled the Southern Kingdom. He followed Hope-Giver with all his heart and soul and strength. Because of this he was given everything his father and father's father had sought: power and popularity, wealth and wisdom and long life.

But in his final years he suffered because of his failures.

CHAPTER 4

THE SAILOR KING

Merchants from far away came to the throne of Good King, wishing trading privileges in the Southern Kingdom. Always near, and listening to their stories, was a little boy, the king's son. He enjoyed hearing about the great caravans crossing the desert, but he especially liked meeting the sea-faring travelers with their marvelous tales of courage and curiosity. He had never seen the sea, though his father promised to take him. Such a won-drous place it must be, a highway of rolling water that stretched to the far-thest reaches of the Blue Planet.

"I will be a sailor some day," the boy told his father. The king laughed.

"I have other work in mind for you. You are smart and strong and full of vision. The one who sits on this throne after me will need to be like that. You shall be king."

"Thank you, sir," the little boy said, "but your work does not seem very interesting. I would much rather be a sailor."

Good King rocked with laughter. "I also would like that. But we do have a kingdom that needs looking after. Besides, we don't have a single trading ship. As long as you are here the kingdom will always have at least one sailor."

Years later, Sailor remembered that conversation. He still liked to talk with people of the coastal nations about their ships and trade routes. But he had other concerns. Good King had passed from the Blue Planet.

His father had been right. There was a kingdom that needed a lot of looking after, and he was its king.

Sailor was a good man, who followed the footsteps of Hope-Giver. He had lots of dreams. He wanted to be a strong, worthy king, who defended his borders and brought peace to the land. He built walls and gates and towers. Every major city was fortified, and the City of Palms had never been so impenetrable. He let ambassadors from other lands see his well-trained army and his strong defenses. He wanted them to tremble at such power. They did.

The new king became rich and popular. He was a king of great ambition. One of his many dreams was that the divided kingdoms would know peace. For generations the Southern Kingdom had been separated from the Northern Kingdom. Many soldiers had died in their wars. But who even remembered why the nations had moved apart or why they fought so much?

"We should repair this tear," he told a close friend one day, a keeper of the Special Place. "We are brothers. I shall not try to unite our countries by shedding blood and conquering land. The way to bring unity is to put away swords and talk to one another."

"It is a good dream, but the time is not now," his friend told him. "The Northern Kingdom has become a dark and difficult and hostile place. They honor Shining One. They are cruel and cunning and untrustworthy."

Sailor King sighed. "Perhaps I will never see the kingdom as it was in the days of Wise King. But we need to remind the Northern King that we are brothers and that they can again turn to Hope-Giver. We can take first steps."

"Then I will talk much with Hope-Giver for you," said the keeper of the Special Place, "for I am more afraid of this beautiful dream of yours than I would be of an invasion of Delta soldiers."

Sailor King found the Northern King warm and agreeable and ready to forge an alliance. *He doesn't follow Hope-Giver,* Sailor King thought, *but he is a fine fellow.*

Sailor King never asked the one who holds the stars in his hands for his blessing or wisdom. If he had, Hope-Giver would have told him that the charming king on the northern throne was more evil and dedicated to Shining One than was any who had gone before him.

He had sacrificed his own children.

He had fought against the truth-tellers.

He had robbed and murdered.

This king also was weak. The real ruler was his wicked queen. Sailor King and the Northern King entered into an alliance, and the Northern

King gave his daughter to be bride to the son of Sailor King.

Sailor King was very pleased. *Surely this will bring our peoples back together,* he thought. The people of both kingdoms were also pleased by the splendid wedding feast from which food was sent throughout the land.

But Hope-Giver turned his face away in anger.

Long afterward, when wildflowers mingled with spring harvests, the Southern King traveled to the capital of the Northern Kingdom. The city was beautiful as it rested on an oval hilltop behind the strength of three mighty walls. The royal palace was two stories high, its walls inlaid with so much ivory that it was called the ivory palace.

The kings and nobles were served lavishly on gold and silver. As the night grew long and the wine low, the Northern King stood. "Through the years of our alliance, it has never been tested in battle," he said in an expansive, inebriated speech.

"It is almost a shame that we are not at war with anyone," responded the Southern King.

"Then let us begin one. Long ago the king of the City of Caravans took the City of Refuge. Let's cross the Winding River and take it back. Our Kingdoms will once again act as one."

It seemed a splendid suggestion. "But I will ask Hope-Giver whether he will go with us."

"Oh, I have wise followers of the one beyond the sky to ask," said the Northern King. "They will tell us all we need to know."

Four hundred keepers gathered before the kings, but they did not have the look of keepers of the Special Place for Hope-Giver. They were of Shining One's temples.

"Shall we be successful if we go to war?" asked the Northern King.

The dark keepers were enthusiastic. "Go, and you shall win great glory in the destruction of your enemies."

The Southern King turned to his host. "These men seem quite optimistic, but I wish to speak with one who knows the words of Hope-Giver."

The Northern King gave a look of disgust. "Oh, we have one of those, a young man who comes out of the hills to give me disagreeable words from the one who holds stars in his hands. But I prefer these reports."

"Nevertheless, I would like to hear this man."

A runner was sent to the mountains. Many hours later a young man in rugged clothes bowed before the two kings.

"Shall we go to war?" asked the Northern King.

"You have people to ask. If they tell you to go, then go. You do not want to listen to me."

"But I do," said the Southern King.

"Then hear what Hope-Giver has shown me of this battle. I saw your soldiers scattered across the hills like sheep. Hope-Giver looked upon them with sorrow and said, 'Since you have no leader, go home in peace.'"

The Northern King pounded his fist in anger. "Listen to his bad report!"

"But is it true?" asked the Southern King, and saw the sparkle of Hope-Giver's presence in the young man's face.

"The time of judgment has come," said the speaker. He turned to the Northern King. "You have your alliance. Now Shining One has made such an alliance with Hope-Giver. He has agreed to lure you to your death for your crimes."

The Southern King did not like the words. The Northern King hated them. He ordered the young man bound and held as a criminal. Either might have willingly put aside the battle plan, but it had become a matter of honor. They assembled their army and crossed the Winding River.

The Northern King feigned disinterest in the words of the truth-teller. But he was obviously shaken. When the battle approached he disguised himself as a simple warrior. Southern King wore his royal battle robe and armor.

The king of the City of Caravans had a plan. His outnumbered foot soldiers would strike together with as much strength as possible. Meanwhile the chariots would sweep across the field, searching for the Northern King.

The armies struck with a great roar and clash. Almost immediately the chariot warriors converged on the royal robe they saw in the midst of battle. They raised their swords and cut off his ways of escape. Southern King looked beyond the sky, knowing that he was about to die. But the chariot warriors looked into his eyes and pulled back from him. They had seen that he was not the Northern King.

Yet the battle continued.

Swords clashed and sparked and drew blood.

Arrows flew from tight-strung bows.

In the midst of the fighting a cry of woe came from the soldiers of the

Northern King. One of their fallen comrades was quickly carried from the field, a fatal arrow still imbedded deep in his chest.

With a final gasp, the body of Northern King lay cold and still.

In the end the City of Refuge was reclaimed, and the Southern King returned to his palace victorious but saddened and humbled. The keeper of the Special Place confronted him: "Beware of alliances with those who follow different paths. Why join forces with one who hates the maker of all?"

The king saw the futility and folly of his dream. He begged forgiveness for not submitting it to Hope-Giver. He pledged his heart and soul and strength to the one who holds stars in his hands, and his love for Hope-Giver grew deeper. The Southern King led his kingdom along the path of goodness and justice and faith. Hope-Giver touched the land and it blossomed.

One dream the king still harbored, clutching it deep in his heart, was that ships would someday sail upon the Great Sea under his banner.

He invited shipbuilders and merchants from faraway kingdoms to his palace. He listened once more to their tales of adventure on the high sea and voyages to exotic coasts. But all his dreams were beyond his reach, for he had no ship or harbor or access to a deep waterway.

But then an immense invasion burst upon the New Land, threatening to sweep away the entire kingdom. Instead of giving in to fear, the king called the people to lift their faces beyond the sky. They listened to the words of Hope-Giver and sang on the way to the battle and utterly defeated their enemy.

The kingdom received wealth and weapons and land from the defeated kings. Included in the land was a section of seacoast with the very seafaring port from which Wise King's trading ships had once sailed.

His goal was in reach, but Southern King was uncertain what to do. He could rebuild the port, but he still lacked a fleet of trading vessels that could call this harbor home. Once again the king failed to take his problem to Hope-Giver, because he had never given this dream to the one above all. He was afraid of what the answer might be.

The Southern King again turned to the Northern King and said, "Let us join to build a trading empire that will bring silver and gold, ebony and ivory, precious stones and rare goods. We shall become more wealthy and prosperous than ever before."

The Northern King had less interest in ships but more in becoming wealthy. Together they invested in the finest fleet to sail the Tropical Ocean. Sailor King had earned his name.

At the moment of triumph, a truth-teller came to Sailor King.

"Hope-Giver asks why you again join with those who hate him. He will not allow this alliance to proceed. Because you did not give your dream to him, he will take it from you."

Early the next morning a powerful storm slammed into the new fleet. Mighty winds drove the beautiful ships upon the rocky shore. Waves tore them apart.

Bows were broken.

Hulls were breached.

Ships were battered until they sunk.

Not one ship of the fleet would ever set sail. Sailor King sat on the shore looking at the wreckage and wept. He accepted the judgment, but he was never the same.

A few summers later, he lay down at dusk and never awoke.

A servant of the palace said that late that night he saw a silver ship sail across a starry canopy and fade beyond the sky on the steady winds of eternity.

On board, Sailor King waved good-bye, a true sailor at last.

A DARK HEART
HAS MANY DREAMS,
BUT NONE LEAD TO LIGHT.

CHAPTER 5

THE WICKED QUEEN

It was the way of kings to seal alliances with marriage. The fondest dream of Sailor King was to reunite the divided halves of the realm of Wise King. For his alliance with the Northern Kingdom he proposed that his firstborn prince be wed to the princess of the North. She would come to be the Southern Queen. He was sure Hope-Giver would bless such a plan.

But Sailor King's dreams were not those of Hope-Giver. The royal family of the north was one of the most wicked that the Blue Planet had yet known. No, this joining would cause much suffering.

Shining One saw that finally he could fully control both kingdoms. Here at last were the instruments he needed to conquer the People of the Promise. Through the wicked dynasty of the North and the young bride in the South, he would plunder hope from both kingdoms.

The king and his firstborn son were delighted with the princess. She was beautiful and cultured and impressed visitors of every rank. She was all that a queen should be. She also was strong-willed and haughty and devious, as a pampered princess was allowed to be.

Like the rest of her family, the princess had made Shining One her tutor and friend and constant companion. He taught her the secrets of greed and violence and anarchy. Those who stood in her way were very sorry. None stood in her way if they could help it.

Her first taste of power came when Sailor King left the City of Palms to supervise the building of his trading ships. His firstborn was given charge of the kingdom. The son would defend the land while his father built for it a trading empire. But the ships were destroyed and the empire came to naught and the king soon died. His body was entombed and his oldest son sat alone on the golden throne.

Shining One smiled.

The princess laughed.

Followers of the one beyond the sky trembled.

All too soon it was obvious that this king and his wife would bring trouble. The new king reveled in his power and listened intently to his wife's whisperings. Now she would take back the wealth of Sailor King. Now she would destroy the influence of Hope-Giver in the king's councils.

"I have news for the king alone," she said one day, interrupting an audience. When they were alone she called into the chamber a little man who looked none in the face. He nervously explained that he was a servant of one of the king's brothers. Late one night he had served all of the brothers and certain other leaders of the nation. They met to plot, he said, to take the kingdom and kill its king.

"What will I do if my family stands together against me?" the king stammered, wringing his hands.

"We could have them arrested for their crimes," the queen responded, "though their intentions might be hard to prove." She glanced at the little man.

"If it p–p–please my master," he put in, "I know g–good men who would risk all at your service. They have some small ability with the sword. They would be your champions."

"This is good news, my husband," the queen said quickly. "Allow me to meet with these patriots, while you return to your work."

That night death burst into the homes of the king's brothers, as well as the houses of high counselors who represented Hope-Giver. Assassins cut down each man and each wife and every child. As soon as the bodies were in their tombs, the queen claimed all that they owned for the king's treasury. The king spoke publicly now about a dark conspiracy that loyal men had stopped. However, the City of Palms and the countryside whispered of another sort of conspiracy.

The queen herself took the places of the slain advisors. In a few cycles of the moon she had swept away all the good done by the king's beloved father.

Craftsmen built new temples to Shining One.

Everywhere, altars honored the serpent.

Unspeakable things were done in the shadow of the snake.

The Southern Kingdom was as deceived as its northern brothers. The Wayward King refused to look beyond the sky or to listen to the wind. The timeless stories and forever truths were discarded. A cynical people turned from Hope-Giver.

The one who held stars in his hands ached at all he saw. He had promised not to destroy the house of Shepherd King, though he knew he must judge the Wayward King and his people. He also knew what Shining One refused to accept. One day he would bring the kingdom back to him, at least for a time. For now he simply removed his shield of protection.

First the slashing blades of the People of the Desert reclaimed the land that Sailor King had taken from them. They almost reached the Valley of Apples before they were turned back by Wayward King and his warriors.

Not long afterward a messenger approached the king with a sealed scroll in his hand.

"I have been sent by the truth-teller who speaks for Hope-Giver. He is the most respected seer of the two kingdoms."

"Read his words!" demanded the king.

"These are not his words," said the messenger, "but the words of Hope-Giver. You can hide nothing from his eyes. He has seen how you left your father's way and soaked the soil with the innocent blood of your brothers. Now Hope-Giver has sent the People of the Desert, but you have not looked to him. You have felt no grief for your evil."

"Take these words from my presence!" yelled Wayward King, grasping and tearing the scroll. But the messenger went on as if he still read from it.

"The maker of all will open your eyes with tears and humble your heart with agony. You have listened to your wicked wife, so he shall take your wives and children. You have brought sickness to your kingdom, so a lingering sickness will eat away your insides until you scream for death. Then you may understand what you have done."

The Wicked Queen had been sitting expressionless. The serpent coiled at her feet gave an occasional twitch. Now she turned calmly to the guards. "Strike him down."

"No!"

The king's voice cut through the room, and the guards stopped.

"Return to your master," he told the messenger. "Tell him we shall see if these words have teeth."

The next spring the People of the Sea joined the people from the headwaters of the Wide River. Intent on revenge for past wars, they ravaged the land and seized cities and struck down people. They gathered at the impenetrable walls of the City of Palms itself and found a way to breach a weak gate. The king's soldiers laid down their arms in humiliation.

The enemy stripped the palace of silver and gold.

They burned and plundered the great city.

They took away the king's wives and children.

In the midst of the battle, Wayward King took hold of Wicked Queen in his right hand and their youngest son in his left. They hid in the water tunnels leading to the bubbling springs. Thus three of the royal family survived. None of the rest was heard from again.

Wayward King faced a ruined city and a devastated people. Much of his bloody wealth had been carried away. What remained was needed to replace and restore and rebuild.

He no longer took his ease in the coolness and glory of the great council chamber. He instead listened to the cries of grief from the city and walked the streets with builders. He felt ashamed but not humbled, and he did not turn to the one above all.

One day he stood with his advisors by a ruined section of wall, where great stones had been toppled in.

"Why can't we get more workers from the villages? There is too much work to do. The cost is too great."

An advisor shook his head.

"The villages have buried many and must repair buildings and replace crops. They suffer worse than we. It is as if the Sea People and Headwaters People took a great knife and split us open."

Suddenly it seemed as if that was what was happening to the king, for he doubled over to his knees and then writhed amid the rubble of the ground.

The pain seemed beyond enduring. Healers came and went, shaking their heads. Never had they seen such misery. The pain was sharp and stabbing and constant. Nothing eased the suffering.

"This is no ordinary sickness," one of them whispered. "Death has filled his body, yet he does not die."

"It is the sickness of judgment," agreed her companion.

Wicked Queen called the priests of Shining One, but their care seemed to leave the king in greater misery.

Days became months, and he thought much of the words of Hope-Giver. He was tasting what his nation would suffer because of him. This was now just one more agony he must endure, for he was not humbled. After a year of anguish and pain, Hope-Giver released the king's body to Shining One.

Those who knew of his torments were relieved that his pain was over, but they did not grieve. No one mourned his passing, not even the Wicked Queen. She was too busy preparing her son to follow the path of his father.

At twenty-two summers the son became king. He had been taught well the secrets of Shining One. He held fast to his mother's path of greed and violence and anarchy. He was no more than settled upon his throne when his uncle, the king of the north, cried for help. "Do not hesitate to go," said his mother. "The kingdom will be safe in my hands."

The king of the City of Caravans had again invaded the land, the very man who had killed the father of Wicked Queen. Now was the time for revenge, to strike the one who had struck his grandfather.

The Southern King fought beside his uncle with courage until an enemy blade cut into the Northern King's side. The old king was taken quickly from the battlefield on the east bank to his summer palace in the Valley of Harvest. After the victory had been won, the Southern King went to the bedside of his uncle and stayed with him while he recovered. Together they walked the city, speaking of the future of their kingdoms—a future that neither would see.

**FOR INNOCENCE TO SURVIVE,
COURAGE MUST TAKE ACTION.**

CHAPTER 6

THE BOY KING

Horsemen are coming!" shouted the watchmen from their towers in the summer capital of the Northern Kingdom. The kings of the North and South, uncle and nephew, were together on the wall, watching a distant party of horsemen fly through the Valley of Harvest.

The Northern King smiled and pointed to the man leading the charging horses.

"The one in front who rides so wildly is the commander of my armies. They will take some time yet arriving. Shall we take two chariots and join them?"

The horses were nearby, so soon the kings rambled through the city gates. Then they gave their proud chargers their heads and felt the wind blow over their hair.

They did not notice the mournful melody that moved slowly toward them.

"What is the news?" the Northern King called out as he reined up before the horsemen. When he saw the looks of death on their faces he turned white. "Are we at peace?" he asked.

"Peace?" spat the commander and drew his bow from its scabbard. "Not when a kingdom revels in the death and despair of Shining One!"

Too late the king realized what the words meant.

"Flee!" he screamed to the king on the other chariot as he turned his horses about. "It's treason! You must. . ."

The Northern King sank to the floor of his chariot, an arrow piercing his heart. The Southern King was farther away and lashed his horses in terror toward the open gates, which now seemed very distant. So fast he rode that the archers could not use their skill. Arrows flew wildly by. He felt a fire of pain go through his shoulder, but he reached the gates in safety.

"Guards," he screamed. "Rebels have struck your king. To arms."

Almost immediately the guards were there, armed and ready. They steadied the horses and helped the king from his chariot. But the gates did not close against the horsemen, nor did anyone move the Southern King to safety. Instead he found himself looking in the cold, clear eyes of the commander.

Wicked Queen sat on the throne and heard the news of how her brother, king of the North, and her son, king of the South, had been savagely struck down. She sat still, almost as still as a serpentine statue, expressing no mourning or sorrow or anger.

"Assemble all his male children, and I will go to them," she said quietly.

The section of the house reserved for the king's wives and children was surprised that the mother of the king wanted to see all her grandsons. But the daughter of Wicked Queen was quite concerned by such a demand.

My mother has never shown any love toward these children, she thought to herself. *And why the sons only, unless something has happened to my brother the king? But why all of them, unless. . .*

A horrible thought gripped her, and she looked quickly around to see who had not yet assembled. The youngest toddler had been fussy all morning with teething, and his nurse was still trying to dress him.

"He is in no mood for an audience with the queen," she joked. "Let's not send him or he will disrupt everything."

"But, mistress, the demand was most insistent."

"Nevertheless, he won't be missed. I know a room that is far out of the way. We will do our best to keep him calm and content."

The queen passed quickly into the room with the children, surrounded by mothers and caretakers.

"Are all the children here?" she asked, glancing around with apparent disinterest. It seemed so, she was told.

She turned to the guards, "Kill the children, every one of them. If anyone else gets in your way, kill them as well."

The horrified screams were beginning as she left the room, a smile on her face. Now who would dispute her right to rule?

Of the children of Wicked Queen, the woman hiding the baby had been most tiresome, always a rebel. She had taken to spending time with the followers of Hope-Giver. The queen had been horrified to learn, rather after the fact, that her daughter had actually married one of the keepers of the Special Place. She thought of having him killed. But it likely would do no good.

The girl looked beyond the sky
and walked with the one above all
and hated the evil of Shining One.

The queen had let this rebellious daughter go her own way as long as she didn't cause trouble.

Evening approached and the keeper of the Special Place was becoming anxious. His wife had gone to help with the royal children, as she often did. But she had never been out so late.

Suddenly two women burst into the door, looking over their shoulders in fear. His wife was followed by another who carried a large and squirmy bundle that was loud with protest.

"Have you heard the cries of fear and panic and death?" his wife began. "My mother has done her worst. My brother has died and now she has killed all of her grandsons so she can continue to rule."

"Oh, may Hope-Giver act," he said with a feeling of woe.

"Perhaps he has," said his wife, as a tiny child emerged from the bundle, immediately in a better mood now that he was free. She gently set him on the floor and with a squeal of glee he began to explore.

"Hope-Giver has used you to save the future of his promise. It is like the birth of General, who was hidden from death in the Wide River of the Land of Pyramids."

"What shall we do? Anyone who sees me with a boy child will be suspicious. If word reaches my mother, none of us will be alive tomorrow."

"How did that wicked creature ever have a daughter so wonderful as you?" her husband said with a tender smile. Then he turned to the child's caretaker.

"I have an idea that should provide safety for you and the child, though the surroundings will not be so comfortable as the palace." He moved toward the door. "I must speak with the other keepers of the Special Place."

By morning the woman and child had seemingly vanished from the Blue Planet. Only a few knew that inner storerooms of the magnificent Special Place had suddenly been outfitted as a snug dwelling and nursery.

The child played in the courts of the sanctuary under ever-watchful eyes.

He was taught the ways of Hope-Giver.

He was told the stories of the past.

He was tutored in the art of being a king.

Six summers of misery passed for the Southern Kingdom, in the thrall of the Wicked Queen. Then one day the keeper of the Special Place called together the most trustworthy captains of the army.

"An heir to the throne of Shepherd King lives," he declared.

The words brought utter silence among the assembled soldiers.

"Some of the king's sons actually survived the great massacre?"

"All died on that awful day, except one." A pale-looking young boy was led in.

"Hope-Giver has not left us without hope. He has been as my own son, and I have taught him to cling to the one who holds stars in his hands."

The captains gasped in shock.

"Here is our king," continued the keeper. "Now we must decide how to answer the treachery of Wicked Queen."

For the next few days, the City of Palms kept a closely guarded secret that was spread among those who followed Hope-Giver or who had stood against the queen, some at great cost.

Then all quietly gathered before the Special Place. The palace guard—their swords and spears gleaming—marched to the gate that opened into the sanctuary. The keepers stepped through the gate in their finest robes. Almost totally hidden by all these trappings walked a somber-faced boy who was struggling to understand the significance of what was happening.

The soldiers stood about the boy and the people could see him for the first time. A crowd of curious onlookers gathered to watch.

What was happening here?

Who was this child?

Why was the palace guard protecting him?

The soldiers each bowed their knees and vowed before Hope-Giver to protect their new king with their lives.

The keeper led the boy before the growing crowd, which was suddenly tense with apprehension of what was about to happen. The keeper faced the child with a tremble and a tear.

He placed a crown on his young head.

He handed him a scroll of eternal truth.

He anointed him with oil.

Rams' horns shook the city walls. Cheers were shouted and songs sung as crowds spread through the narrow streets. Everyone danced joyfully before the one above all.

The queen looked out from a window of the palace to see what wondrous thing had happened. A triumphal procession was approaching her royal home, centered around a young boy wearing a golden crown. Some of those about him were members of her royal bodyguard. Her face went ashen. The ancient serpent hissed and spat venom into her ear.

The queen ran to the courtyard, summoning her guards and screaming in a high-pitched hysteria. She ripped her robe and pushed people out of her way. A silver dagger was clutched tightly in her fist. Her eyes glowed with death as she ran toward the Boy King.

A hundred spears barred her way. Strong hands tore the dagger from her fist and held her flailing arms. As the guards took her, she screamed obscenities.

The crowd followed the guards as they took the queen to the edge of the city. There her breath was taken quickly by an expert sword thrust.

A great throng was gathered at the Special Place and the keeper offered spotless, newborn lambs to the one above all. The people bent their knees and humbled their hearts and looked beyond the sky. They pledged to be the people of hope who would always keep their eyes on Hope-Giver. The city was cleansed of anything and anyone used in the worship of Shining One. His temples were destroyed and his altars leveled and his statues shattered.

The people felt a freedom and peace and happiness that had been absent since the days of Sailor King. Wicked Queen was dead and the people rejoiced. They gathered back at the sanctuary courtyard and circled the Boy King. Then the keeper and the guards and the people led the new king to the royal palace. They cheered when he sat upon the golden throne.

The keeper of the Special Place was an ancient man, but he held the hand of Boy King and led him in the ways of Hope-Giver. He watched the child grow tall and strong. The two were dearer to one another than father and son. He was the Boy King's teacher and friend and advisor.

He taught the young one truth in the ancient stories.

He showed him light in the steps of Hope-Giver.

He pointed to the wisdom of walking the highlands.

Twenty peaceful summers passed, until the horrors of Wicked Queen seemed a distant memory. Boy King married and had many children. One morning as he looked from a window of the royal palace, he noticed cracks in the stonework of the Special Place. The sanctuary that had been his refuge was old and had been pillaged and abused. Its wood was rotten and its metal rusty. Its gold was gone and its curtains torn.

"Disgraceful," Boy King shook his head. "How could we allow the home of Hope-Giver to look like this?"

So the king ordered all the keepers to go to every town of the Southern Kingdom to collect what was needed to repair and replace and restore.

But so much needed to be done that the giving was not enough, and the work did not proceed.

The king knew that the people had drifted far from Hope-Giver. They no longer looked to his Special Place as their refuge. They must see it for themselves.

"Place a wooden box outside the sanctuary," said the king. Then he sent messengers to every town of the Southern Kingdom.

"Come to the City of Palms.

"See what has become of your Special Place.

"See how far it has descended from its glory."

The people came and saw that their Special Place had lost much of its past beauty, and many wept at their own selfish disregard for Hope-Giver. They filled the box many times over, until there was more than enough. When the work had been done the splendor of the Special Place was as bright as during the days of Wise King.

The old keeper rubbed his dim eyes and stared in amazement. "It is just as I remember it."

A few weeks later the keeper looked beyond the sky and a deep peaceful smile lifted his face. In a heartbeat he went from the house of Hope-Giver on the Blue Planet to his eternal home beyond the sky.

CHAPTER 7

THE MIGHTY THISTLE

For generations, when people of the City of Palms spoke of Boy King, they always divided his life into two parts.

"Oh, I remember when he watched us fill the cracks in the sanctuary wall," said one. "That was shortly before the Trusted Keeper died."

Another might say, "What he did was so unjust. But remember, that was after the Trusted Keeper died."

It was true. The man had listened intently to the counsel of Trusted Keeper and followed Hope-Giver with a ready heart. The same man had refused to hear the words of Trusted Keeper's son and turned his back on the ways of Hope-Giver. They were the same man, but they weren't. People preferred to think of the softhearted boy and not the hard-hearted king. No one knew why the king had turned from Hope-Giver when the aged keeper of the Special Place died. But when his teacher was gone something deep and drastic changed within him. He became cold and moody and cruel. He listened to the words of false advisors. He turned from the beautiful sanctuary to the serpentine statues. He forgot all the truth and followed the lies, even when Hope-Giver removed his shield from the kingdom.

The army suffered bitter defeat in battle against the City of Caravans.

The king was grievously wounded and besieged in his city.

The enemy army stripped away the beauty from the Special Place.

These losses only made the king more embittered. Even his servants came to hate him. They had seen the heart of Boy King grow hard after the death of the Trusted Keeper. They had watched him order the stoning of Trusted Keeper's son. They had seen the magnificent temple stripped.

"This king is bringing death upon our people," whispered a small group of plotters. They decided that they would instead bring death upon the king. Trusted servants slipped into his royal bedchamber.

A silver dagger.

A thrust to the chest.

A gasp of death.

The king never rose from his bed and his servants slipped into the shadows. It had been so easy.

"How could they have done such a thing?" cried the king's son.

The firstborn son had seen twenty-five summers. He remembered the good days when his father listened to Trusted Keeper and looked beyond the sky. He remembered when his father had rebuilt and restored and repaired the splendid Special Place. His father had lost his way, but the son still loved him.

The killers had expected the son to be secretly grateful and find some way to quietly reward them. So they did not hold their dark act in silence. Rather, they boasted of it, and soon found themselves dragged before the new king.

The son placed the edge of his own sword to their quivering throats. "To kill a king anointed by Hope-Giver is no light matter."

The two were silent.

"I should kill you and all your sons," said the new king. "But I will not shorten the days of your sons." With a quick movement of his sword he brought justice on the murderers. Then he went to the sanctuary and sacrificed a spotless, newborn lamb to the one above all.

As the smoke rose, he looked up. "Oh, Hope-Giver, help me be a king who can honor you in everything I do."

Once again a king committed all his heart and soul and strength. Once again, as the sun touched the Mountains of the Dawn, a king walked the misty highlands. Once again a king studied the sacred scrolls.

The warriors of the People of the Desert were again causing suffering in the Southern Kingdom. The time had come to act. The Southern King wanted his people to respect him as a man of valor and a conquering king. He called together an army. He trained them with sword and spear and shield. He readied his kingdom for war. His army was strong, but the People of the Desert were fierce fighters. Could he stand against them?

He sent a hundred bars of silver to the king of the North, asking for all the soldiers his silver would buy.

Now he had a mighty army. Now he would be a conquering king.

But Hope-Giver sent a truth-teller to the camp.

"I must be mistaken," the truth-teller said to the king when they had embraced. "Your army seems so fine and large. I thought I saw banners of the Northern Kingdom. But you would not do such a thing?" asked a man of truth.

"I have made no alliance," said the king hesitantly.

"So there are no warriors of that army here?"

"You know there are some," the king snapped, not looking his friend in the eye. "We are preparing to attack the People of the Desert, a fierce and cunning and bloody enemy belonging to Shining One."

"But you have joined hands with men who also walk with Shining One. If you march with them there will be no victory."

The king bowed his face to the ground. "If the one above all wishes me to fight without additional soldiers, so be it. I will not question one who is infinite and eternal and all-powerful."

So the king sent the Northern Army's warriors home without seeing battle or tasting the victory or taking the spoils of war that would enrich them.

They were humiliated.

They burned with rage.

They swore revenge.

Then the king marshaled his strength and faced south. In the Valley of Salt he saw the power of the Desert People—and he smashed it.

The soldiers of the Southern Kingdom named their leader Conquering King. Much land was taken and much plunder collected. The seaport of Sailor King was captured once more. So were several golden images of the ancient snake. It was custom to take such statues to one's own palace as a reminder of the victory won. Conquering King set them in prominent places and became fascinated with them. Often he would stop and gaze at them in their awful magnificence. Slowly he was becoming confused and darkened of mind. Rather than go to the Special Place, he went to the statues and bowed to them and offered sacrifices.

Hope-Giver sent the truth-teller once more. This time there was no joyful greeting, and an oppressive darkness hung about the audience chamber that the torches could not dispel.

"Who is it that gave you victory against the Desert People? Who ended their threat?"

"And who is now called Conquering King? I recognize the hand of Hope-Giver. He should see that my hand also vanquished my enemy."

"The face of evil is seducing you."

"You have no right to speak to your king in such a manner."

The truth-teller slowly turned his back on the king and began walking away. Then he turned and in a quiet voice spoke once more. "Those who look beyond the sky will know victory. Those who bow to Shining One will know defeat."

At that moment the king was told of a messenger at his gate.

"The northern troops you sent home have turned against us," the messenger said. "They have crossed our border as a war band to raid our cities."

The Southern King sent a challenge to the Northern King. "If you want a battle, come and meet me face-to-face."

Soon another messenger stood at the gate. This man was from the Northern King.

"My master has sent me to you with a story:

"A thistle with sharp thorns and flowers of purple towered over a field of dry grass. He thought himself great until he saw at the edge of the field a mighty cedar as tall as the sky. The thistle sent a message to the cedar: 'Give your daughter to my son in marriage.'

"But before the cedar could respond, a wild lion wandered through the field. Without noticing, it tread on the thistle. The fragile stalk was broken and the purple flower trampled."

"This story is a great insult to my kingdom," said the Conquering King with wrath in his eye. "We have defeated the Desert People and our kingdom is again great. We will teach you the difference between a thistle and a cedar."

When the Northern King received this message he readied his troops for war. "If Conquering King wishes a battle, a battle he shall have."

Watchers reported the coming of the Northern Army to Conquering King, and in glory he led his army out the gates of the City of Palms.

When the two armies faced each other, many old wounds and insults and betrayals were remembered. The Northern King yelled the charge and the armies collided with such a ferocity that the earth shuddered.

"Stand firm!" yelled Conquering King.

It was too late. Panic was everywhere. Soldiers fled the field to hide in the highland caves and chasms. Conquering King was quickly captured.

The Northern Army marched to the City of Palms and besieged it. They knew of a weak place in the northwest wall and they rammed it until the weak foundation stones were dislodged. Mortar crumbled and the wall fell.

Once again an enemy robbed the Special Place.

The treasures of the palace were taken away.

The golden images of Shining One were removed.

The enemy king captured many leaders of the Southern Kingdom and loaded their backs with riches and marched them toward the northern capital. At the front of these new slaves was Conquering King. He shuffled along with head bent low, sweating beneath the weight of a large golden image of a serpent.

For nine long summers the Southern King was locked in a dark stone prison near the ivory palace. He sat alone on the dirty floor with little to eat. He longed for the days when he had walked with Hope-Giver. Why had he set up the golden images in his palace? Why had he bowed to them?

It was as if the answer came from his old friend, the truth-teller.

"Wake up and weep. Return to Hope-Giver with all your heart and he will embrace you. For he is good and gracious and full of mercy. If you do not return, a ram's horn will blow. The land will tremble. A day of darkness will come."

But another old friend had slithered into his room with very different words:

"If Hope-Giver is good and gracious and full of mercy, why are you in such a place? Listen to my voice. I will give you all the desires of your heart."

Conquering King made his choice, and his heart grew hard toward Hope-Giver.

When the Northern King breathed his last, Conquering King was allowed to return to the City of Palms. He was ragged and wasted and wrinkled.

For fifteen more years Conquering King reigned. Yet as each summer passed his words became more bitter and his ways more wicked. Large golden statues of the serpent could now be seen throughout the city.

"What has happened to your heart?" asked the king's son. "It has turned so dark."

"There is nothing wrong with my heart."

"But you walked with Hope-Giver and asked him to help you be a king of honor."

For a moment he remembered the young vows he had taken. Then the view faded.

"That was long ago." He turned his back on his son and went to the palace window. His eyes blazed and his mind filled with venom. "Hope-Giver abandoned me. Now all the people will abandon him. Make it a decree. Send it through the countryside. I bow before Shining One and command all my people to do the same."

News of this edict traveled fast, and before it could be issued a large mob gathered before the king's palace. The king was forced to flee his own people. Two frightful days' journey to the south, Conquering King was found. He was killed by faithful men who refused to bow before Shining One.

The Southern Kingdom turned once more to Hope-Giver. They destroyed the golden statues and sacrificed spotless, newborn lambs to the one above all.

As the people watched the smoke lift skyward, a light rain dampened their faces. The sun burst through the clouds and a beautiful rainbow arched from the earth into the sky.

Conquering King's son spoke to those who had gathered before the Special Place.

"Before my father was seduced by Shining One, he told me the sacred stories of Hope-Giver. I will now tell you again the story of the rainbow.

"It is a promise to us all:

"For he is always close and will always care."

The people cheered.

EPILOGUE

The man with a hundred wrinkles had set out the table again, and the torches, and the beautiful parchment map. Again the people took turns looking at it to see all the places the stories had described. How many battles had been fought for this land. How tragic that the beautiful New Land had been cut in two because people sided with Shining One.

The small girl approached the man with the long, gray beard.

"It is hard to be a king, isn't it?"

"I suppose it must be. But it could have been easier for the kings and queens I told you about."

"If they had been good instead of bad? Why did they want to be bad?"

"Do you think they wanted to be bad kings? Most of them really wanted to do the right and good and courageous thing. . ." the old man said.

"Yes, that's what I want to do," interrupted the girl. "I want to do the right thing."

"Do you know something they did not know about how to do it?"

"Uh, I know I must walk each day with the one who holds stars in his hands."

"And when the walk is hard?"

"I'll sit down and rest and look at the rainbows."

"What if you can't see any?"

"Oh, Grandfather. You said there are always rainbows. All we need to do is remember the promises of Hope-Giver."

"Yes," said the old man with a smile. "I did say that, didn't I?"

PART 3
THE TRUTH-HOLDER

TABLE OF CONTENTS
THE TRUTH-HOLDER

PROLOGUE

"We have heard some stories of the Southern Kingdom," said the old story-teller to his circle of listeners. He carefully unrolled the parchment map and for a moment seemed unaware of the staring circle and desert night and flickering flame. His ancient eyes studied the valleys and rivers and mountains of the New Land. Looking back to them he said, "The Southern Kingdom fell far from its beginnings under Shepherd and Wise King. But there were some kings who followed Hope-Giver, at least some of the time."

"But what about up here, in the northern half of the New Land?" came a voice from the circle.

"Those were the evil people," said one of the women.

"There were some awful kings," the old man agreed. "But the people really weren't much different from their southern relatives. And they weren't much different than us."

"They had more troubles, didn't they?" the woman asked.

"They broke from Wise King and turned from the Shepherd dynasty and left the beautiful sanctuary behind. When they did that they were ready to be drawn to the lies of Shining One."

A few in the circle bent their heads in sorrow.

"So they seldom used the name Hope-Giver," said the storyteller as he stepped closer to the fire. "They followed the lie, so he gave them a name to fit the work he had to do among them. That name was Truth-Holder."

CHAPTER 1

THE DYNASTY OF THE CALF

W ise King has passed beyond the sky."

It was desert hot and desert dry in the Land of the Delta. A small community of the People of the Promise lived there, tradesmen and merchants and shepherds who stayed to themselves. Most were from the northern part of the New Land and so lived with the young man called Challenger. He had the rippling, muscular build of a champion among warriors. He was the son of a line of elders and had a noble bearing.

The messengers had risked the dangers of the wilderness and had traveled many days to stand before this man, who carried the promise that one day he would be king. Wise King had feared him as a dangerous revolutionary and chased him from his kingdom.

But Wise King ruled no longer.

"Who will take the throne when the days of mourning are passed?" the Challenger asked.

"Chosen Son will soon be crowned."

"Will the northern elders follow him?"

"They fear he lacks discretion. They want you by their side when they face him. Will you come?"

The price was high for the fine white stallion bred by the People of the Pyramids. This mount had the stamina to travel quickly through the harsh wilderness. Challenger paid in silver without hesitation. He covered himself in the robes of the desert traveler to protect himself from the burning sun. For three hard days he urged the stallion north by sun and moon, stopping only to water and rest his mount before pushing on.

"You promised that you would give to me the northern tribes," shouted the young man at the sky. "Help me claim that crown."

"You shall rule the North," whistled the wind in his ears. "Wise King's son shall rule the South."

"Would it not be better if I ruled all?"

"You shall have no more and no less than I have promised."

The lone rider was protected from the heat and robbers through all his hard journey, and on his magnificent horse he made great speed. As he dismounted he learned that the elders were preparing to face the new king.

"Chosen King has been crowned. We offered to follow him if he would treat us and our people fairly," one of the elders explained to the Challenger. "He has refused. He will not give justice to our people. Today we are summoned before him, and we are afraid."

"I am willing to stand with you as your advocate. Are you willing to submit to my leadership, whatever happens?" the Challenger asked pointedly, testing the mettle of the elders.

"We are your people."

First the elders approached in shaking fear before their young and petulant king. Then a darkly robed and hooded traveler stepped from their midst. He pulled off his outer garments to reveal the armor and great sword of a fierce warrior. The move was bold, but he knew that anything less than supreme confidence would cause the nervous elders at his side to falter.

"Oh, great king," he said, addressing the youth who sat on the throne. "We are pleased that you have listened to our plea for relief. We thank you for giving us a definite answer so that we might come to you now with our decision."

"Your decision? I have summoned you to hear what I have decided. . . ."

"Yes, king, we will hold you in suspense no longer. We of the northern tribes decline your gracious offer to rule over us. The southern people can decide for themselves, though we are willing to take them under our wings to protect them from brutal rulers."

The guards standing all around looked to the king, waiting for the order to strike down each of these rebels. The king himself was white with rage and shock and confusion. He had expected to intimidate. Instead he stood in the shadow of this bold stranger.

"Who are you to dare. . . ? My father chose me to wear this crown. I am the grandson of Shepherd, whose family will reign forever." Turning to the elders, the king tried a new approach. "I have been crowned by all the people. What council has established the throne of this peasant traitor?"

The brash warrior answered for the elders. "No council. I was chosen by the one above all, who holds stars in his hands. Your father bowed to King-Maker. But now King-Maker finds you unworthy and has given this people to another. He has given it to me," said the Challenger with brazen confidence. "King-Maker has given me the tribes of the North, and I will take the South as well."

The crowd was wild and ready to riot, northerners against southerners. But before that could happen, Challenger swept his robe from the ground and turned from Chosen King and walked steadily through the people. If the elders did not follow he knew that he was dead. The elders, though, had found their courage and surrounded him in his march—a human shield.

"Will you be our new king?" they asked.

"This day you elders have been wise and bold and risked all to represent your people," answered the Challenger. "If you are willing to entrust those people to me, I am humbled. Together we will give the northern tribes a better future."

Finest gold was purified and melted and poured. Craftsmen set a breathtakingly beautiful crown with jewels. The elders placed it on the head of the young man, and the people stood in awe as he passed before them on his white stallion. It was a day of great celebration throughout the North, the beginning of a kingdom and of a king. There was dancing and singing and feasting deep into the night.

There was much to do, but the new Northern King was an able administrator who knew how to grasp and hold a people's loyalty. He quickly secured his southern boundaries from the attacks of their kinsmen and declared the City of Oaks his capital.

He strengthened its walls.

He reinforced its gates.

He built a palace of limestone and cedar.

King-Maker had been so good to the People of the North. They had freedom from the kings of the South. Word had come that the Southern King was raising an army against them, but no invaders crossed their border. There was peace and prosperity.

In fact, the goodness of King-Maker was the first problem for the new king. At the approach of the special days of worship his outposts on the southern roads reported that great caravans of people headed south, herding their sacrifices of thanksgiving and praise and repentance toward the magnificent sanctuary in the City of Palms.

"They walk into the arms of our enemy," Challenger said in agitated frustration to his advisors.

"But they return when they have worshiped in the sanctuary," said a white-bearded elder. "Why should they not, for there is no war between us and the People of the South? They have allowed us to take our leave."

"Yes," said the king, "and now they woo the hearts of the people back. What have we like the great City of Palms and all its marvelous beauty? That is why they have sent no army against us. Why should they, when the people wander back on their own? Do you wonder what will happen to us who have rebelled against them if the unity is restored?"

A worried advisor saw the point, then wondered aloud: "How can we order the people not to go to their sanctuary?"

Another smiled a sly grin and held up a hand to calm his brethren. "Peace. We approach this from the wrong direction. Don't you see that we are unfair to our people? Why must they walk all the way to the City of Palms to worship? They need their very own Special Places here where they can sacrifice their spotless, newborn lambs."

"Yes," agreed the king in excitement, "we have been remiss. For such a large country we should raise more than one temple, where worship is bright and exciting and easy!"

The best craftsmen in the land made two golden calves, life-sized statues that glowed in the sun with elegance and beauty. The king ran his hand over the burnished metal. He had no Ark of Mystery, but these would do.

One calf was set a day south at the Place of the Portal, where Wrestler had seen the angels of God so many hundreds of summers before. The other was set three days north in the shadow of a snowcapped mountain at the City of Lions. Each calf was set on a stone pedestal and a temple was built around it. Keepers were appointed for each calf. Altars in the temples received the sacrifices of the people. The men of the North brought their spotless, newborn lambs to the golden statue closest to their home. They looked at it in wonder and brought their wives and children to see it. They could not see King-Maker. They were not allowed to see his Ark of Mystery, which was hidden in the inner chamber of the sanctuary. But here were special reminders of King-Maker that one could see and bow before and keep in memory when asking favors of the one above all.

The king came to the Place of the Portal to offer his first sacrifices. As smoke ascended, a bearded truth-teller from the Southern Kingdom pushed through the crowd of onlookers.

He looked at the beautiful statue.

He looked at the king.

He looked at the people.

"What is this senseless thing to which you sacrifice?"

"No, it is not to the statue that we sacrifice, but to King-Maker," protested the king. "This is a reminder of his presence."

"Then what is that?"

Neither the king nor the people had noticed that a poisonous serpent was resting, coiled about the neck of the statue. It seemed so visible now, and it hissed at the man from the South as if preparing to strike.

But the man ignored the serpent and faced the people.

"The one beyond the sky has sent me to you to tell you of his new name," he said. "You have called him King-Maker, for he is the maker of kings. He has instructed the people of the Southern Kingdom to call him Hope-Giver, for he is their hope now that their kingdom is divided.

"To you he must give another name, for he will give no hope to those who have turned from his truth to worship the lie of Shining One. Instead, the one above the sky will contend with you for the truth. He proclaims himself to be Truth-Holder—the source of all that is. He will defend his honor against you, against your false worship. Look to him and he will forgive. Turn from him to Shining One and he will judge."

The serpent whispered into the ear of the king, "He is from the Southern King, and he has come to destroy all you have built."

The king's face went red with rage. He stretched out his hand, pointing toward the speaker. "Seize him!" he ordered.

But no hand was raised against the truth-teller as he continued: "Truth-Holder shall crush this altar between his fingers."

The king's hand that pointed began to shake. He cried out in pain as his fingers stiffened and his hand shriveled. A wind spun about the king and the altar. Suddenly the altar split, spilling the king's sacrifices into the dirt.

The people standing around the golden calf almost trampled one another as they fell back in fear.

Their king was crippled.

Their altar was broken.

Their sacrifices were nothing.

Were the words of the southern man true? Was their new statue so offensive that the one above all would turn from them?

"Help me," the king begged. "Ask Truth-Holder to give me back my hand. Ask him to take away my pain."

The truth-teller looked beyond the sky: "So that this people might know that you hold the truth, give this king grace."

The wind stopped.

The hand relaxed and was whole.

The people gasped in amazement.

The king ran to the truth-teller, embracing him in gratitude. Emotion choked his words. "Forgive my anger. Come to my palace and let us feast, for I owe you much. I shall give you great gifts in appreciation for your act of mercy."

The truth-teller, however, moved away from the king. "I am ordered not to accept anything from you. You are grateful that your hand was restored. Yet you do not look beyond the sky and weep at your wrong and shatter your golden statues. Truth-Holder longs to bless the North, but instead the dynasty of the calf will fall."

Again the king's face was red with rage.

But he did not stretch out his hand.

He did not speak.

PRIDE CLAIMS OPPORTUNITY
AS THE PROPERTY OF ITS FINDER;
HUMILITY LOOKS AROUND
TO FIND ITS SUITABLE OWNER.

CHAPTER 2

THE DYNASTY OF THE NIGHT

The Challenger's heart remained hard. He laid ambitious plans without Truth-Holder.

"I shall be father of a great dynasty," said the king. He had journeyed to the Place of the Portal and bowed before the statue of the golden calf.

"The dynasty of the calf will rule forever," said the ancient serpent, which had wrapped itself around the neck of the calf. "Yes, your sons will be mighty, as are you."

As these words echoed in the king's mind, a messenger reached him. "Your firstborn son has turned pale and his breath is shallow and his skin is cool to the touch."

The king looked to the golden calf, but the snake was gone. He called the greatest healers, but they could do nothing. Then he remembered the truth-teller who had many summers before declared that he would be king.

The man was now old and blind.

He still looked beyond the sky.

He walked the highland near the Place of Peace.

"Disguise yourself and go to the home of this wise man," suggested the king to his wife. "Take him gifts of bread and cake and honey. Ask him how we can save our child."

His wife did so. But she had not been announced when he said words that pierced her heart.

"Wife of Challenger, listen and repeat the words of Truth-Holder to your evil husband: 'The one who holds stars in his hands made you king, but you have listened to false words and bowed to false forms. My children will be destroyed. Therefore I shall destroy the dynasty of the calf.'"

The king's wife stepped back, "No, it cannot be so. Truth-Holder said that our dynasty shall last always."

"Poor woman, you and your husband are deceived. Now you must pay for the lie. As you return home, your firstborn shall die. Your secondborn will fall to the sword. All who turn away will be cut off."

The wife fled the Place of Peace and rushed to the City of Oaks. Before she had entered his sickroom, her firstborn gasped his last breath.

The following spring the Southern Kingdom finally attacked. "Capture the Place of the Portal and destroy the golden calf," the Southern King told his commanders.

The Army of the North defended it with courage, striking down the Southern King and forcing his army from the land.

But the son of the Southern King became the mighty Warrior King. He returned to avenge his father's death. He captured the Place of the Portal and dragged the golden calf through the dusty streets and buried it, upside-down, in a trash heap.

Several seasons later Warrior King again looked north. "If I could capture their capital, the Northern Kingdom will fall."

This time the Northern King had a far superior army than did the South. They defeated their invaders and took the life of Warrior King. The Place of the Portal was reclaimed.

The golden calf returned to its pedestal.

The people bowed before its altar.

The serpent shivered in ecstasy.

The Northern King was broken and old and tired. He called his second-born to his side. With trembling hands he removed the crown from his gray head and set it upon his son.

Like his father the new king listened to the snake and bowed to the golden calf and hardened his heart to Truth-Holder.

In the second spring of his reign he looked to the setting sun and vowed to destroy the People of the Sea. The king asked a childhood friend to lead the Northern Army against the City on the Ridge, a stronghold and base for war bands. His friend was a bold and strong and winsome leader who demanded loyalty, but was loyal to no one.

As the Northern Army besieged the City on the Ridge, the king's friend won the affection and allegiance of his warriors. He made subtle promises and his men turned on their king. Late one moonless night the false friend slipped into the royal tent with a large double-edged sword strapped to his side.

A slash in the dark.

A thud to the ground.

A groan that faded to silence.

The dynasty of the calf ended as the army placed the golden crown on the head of a new, Dark King, who would lead the evil dynasty of the night.

Dark King turned away from the thick, tall walls of the City on the Ridge. The city's defenders watched in disbelief as their enemy broke camp and faded into the highlands. The walls had not been assaulted.

The Northern Army marched through the day and into the night until they reached the City of Oaks. Soldiers bearing torches burst into the palace, killing the dead king's wife and children. They scattered throughout the city in search of every brother and uncle and cousin of the ruling family. In a night of terror the dynasty of the calf was cut from the land.

The people accepted Dark King. He promised strength and security and prosperity beyond their brothers to the South. Dark King offered spotless, newborn lambs on the altar of Shining One.

As pungent smoke lifted toward the sky, Shining One whispered into Dark King's ear. "You are as powerful as any king this land has seen. Take your men and go south."

So Dark King took his men south into the land of Good King. Beyond the Place of the Portal and half a day north of the City of Palms, Dark King captured the Lofty City. He repaired the walls, building them twice as tall and twice as thick. He set in place a fortified double gate and filled the city with a great warrior garrison.

Good King's heart grew faint as this was reported. His enemy was much too close to his capital. The South called its warriors and also sent runners to the king of the City of Caravans with an urgent request:

"Attack the Northern Kingdom.

"Aim for the City of Lions.

"Threaten the second golden calf."

Thousands of warriors pushed across the northern boundary of the Northern Kingdom toward the City of Lions. Shocked and fearful and pressed to save their city, the soldiers abandoned the Lofty City and rushed north to protect their kingdom. Dark King swore at the sky and journeyed back to his capital, where a truth-teller awaited.

"How went your battle with the South? Has your statue and your snake given victory?" he asked. The king scowled. "Truth-Holder has shown me many things. He has shown me how he raised you from the dust and made you leader of the North. Yet you walk in the way of Shining One. So the dynasty of the night will fall."

"That will not be," said Dark King. "My dynasty shall reign forever."

"So thought the kings of the dynasty of the calf. Yours will end as did theirs."

"You shall die for your insolence!"

"No, I shall live to see your death and the death of your son."

The man of truth calmly walked away and the king stood in stunned silence.

For over twenty summers Dark King struggled to make his kingdom great, but to no avail.

There were many battles, but few victories.

There were plentiful harvests, but little prosperity.

There were colorful festivals, but no joy.

Dark King bowed to the golden calf, and the truth-teller looked beyond the sky.

When the king's eyes grew dim, his son followed in his father's footsteps. Short King was small and pale and no warrior, but he chose two powerful men of war to command his army. One had a humble heart and his soldiers loved him. The other had a proud heart and his soldiers thought him a fool.

"Take your men to the City on the Ridge," said Short King to the humble commander. "Finish the siege my father began. Destroy the city and bring me all its riches."

Short King turned to the proud commander. "Stay with me at my royal palace. Protect us from the Kingdom of the South."

So the humble commander went to war, while the proud commander ate and drank with the king in the royal palace. Many days passed and the proud commander went to the golden calf. He bowed before the statue and coveted the yellow metal that made it shine.

"It can be yours," hissed the snake from the shadows of the small temple. "Follow my ways and I shall give you more than you ever dreamed possible."

That night the proud commander dined with the king in the home of a royal advisor. The king drank much wine. He slurred and staggered and stumbled. As the king weaved from the banquet chamber, the proud one followed. Through a doorway and down a hall and into a private courtyard. There large, powerful hands closed around the Short King's neck.

"The people will celebrate your deed," said the snake as he slithered across the courtyard. "You shall be the greatest king since Shepherd."

There was silence.

"But first," continued the serpent, "you must destroy the king's family before they destroy you."

Before the sun graced the Mountains of the Dawn, all the royal family lay dead in their homes. When the sun had reached its height, the aged truth-teller walked the City of Oaks and approached the procession bearing the body of the king to the tombs.

"The dynasty of the night has followed the dynasty of the calf," he said softly. "There is no future for those who deny the one who is infinite and eternal and all-powerful."

The people were horrified by the proud commander's act of violence, but they accepted his coronation in fear.

No one cheered.

No one applauded.

No one danced in the street.

Proud King knew his reign was not supported by the people. Yet if he could gain the allegiance of the humble commander, he was sure the kingdom would follow.

Runners ran to the City on the Ridge with gentle and flattering and generous words for the humble one. Soldiers ushered the messengers into the commander's tent. Moments later a cry of anger exploded from the tent. Soldiers rushed in to find their leader sitting in anguish with his head buried in his hands.

Finally he spoke.

"The proud commander has killed the king and claimed the crown. He desires our aid to help him establish his reign."

The greatest warriors talked among themselves. "Why should we go to the royal city to help an assassin and a fool? If anyone can crown themselves king, then we will crown one worthy of the honor."

They made a simple circle from the flexible branches of an olive tree and placed it on the humble commander's head.

"No. This is not my right."

"Is it the right of the proud one?" asked his men. "Do you wish our kingdom to be ruled by a fool?"

The humble one was silent.

"We will follow you alone."

They raised swords high in unanimous allegiance.

Three days later the Proud King heard that the humble commander and his army approached the city. At last his kingdom was safe.

Proud King went to the walls and watched the army draw near as if prepared for battle. Leading the way, the humble commander wore a withered crown of interwoven olive branches.

"They have betrayed me!" shouted Proud King in fury. "They have not come to establish my kingdom, but to tear it from my hands.

"Shut the gates!

"Secure the city!

"Man the ramparts!

"No one shall take my kingdom from me. Shining One promised that I would be the greatest of all kings."

The soldiers of the city reluctantly followed the orders. All would have preferred to stand with the army outside the walls. They put up only token resistance when the rest of the army pressed the walls and stormed the gate. In less than a day the humble one breached the gate. His men poured through but found no defenders to give them battle.

Proud King ordered his bodyguards to secure the palace entrances with their lives. He went to the innermost chamber. Smashing the rich furnishings he lit the sacred scrolls that told the history of Shepherd King. The parchment burst into yellow flame and as the paper curled into black ashes, he stared into his future. He fanned the fire and used the broken furniture as kindling. The heat grew intense and sweat poured from the king's body. The wood crackled and smoke clouded the room.

The once proud commander slumped to the floor and wept, "All is lost. Shining One is a liar and a thief."

The palace burned and the guards were forced back by the heat. The humble commander and his warriors joined the palace guards as they hopelessly watched the flames turn the sky yellow and red and black. Then all worked to see that the flames did not spread through the city. As night shrouded the land, the palace lay a giant heap of ash.

No one mourned the death, not even the ancient snake that warmed itself near a blackened crown in the midst of the cooling rubble.

A CASTLE CAN PROVIDE PROTECTION.
IT CAN NEVER PROVIDE HOPE.

CHAPTER 3

THE DYNASTY OF THE CASTLE

The palace was ash and rubble. The surrounding buildings were blackened with the scars of disaster. The fire had swept through the royal district of the city, leaving an ugly mark on the capital.

The people looked to the soldiers.

The soldiers looked to the new king.

The king could look toward no one.

"It is time to leave this place and build a new city," said the king. "The people need a dream, and our capital should have a greatness to be envied by all, with beauty and strength and significance."

The Northern Kingdom rallied around the humble king and cheered his wonderful dream.

The king walked the highlands and valleys, searching for the perfect site on which to build a beautiful city. Atop an oval hill just half a day's journey north of the City of Oaks he found the place where he would lay foundation stones of an impregnable citadel. He bought the land for many pieces of silver. His dreams were drawn on a hundred parchments.

For six summers stonecutters quarried rectangular blocks and slowly moved them to the hilltop, where workers placed them layer upon layer. Triple-thick walls with bulwarks and ramparts and battlements protected a castle stronghold such as would have been the desire of many a king on the Blue Planet.

"Mine is the dynasty of the castle," proclaimed the once humble king. "My sons and grandsons shall reign here. Kings from far lands will journey to see this city and to honor the castle kings."

The Northern King interrupted his work when new raiding parties from the People of the Plains attacked the crops. He conquered them, taking many prisoners who would move more stones to the citadel. The Castle

King also looked south and made peace with the Good King. He looked north and set up trade with the king of the City of Caravans.

Then he looked west to the coastal plains. The People of the Coast were shipbuilders who sailed the Great Sea. They were explorers and traders and artists. They followed Shining One, seeing him as a golden man who rode the clouds with lightning in his hands. He was the source of life and all the people committed themselves to him.

The Northern King made an alliance with the People of the Coast. To seal their relationship the daughter of the Coastal King was given to marry the firstborn son of the Northern King.

"This should not be," said the truth-teller, the one who had predicted the fall of the night dynasty. "Truth-Holder warned our people not to marry those who follow Shining One."

"We can marry whomever we wish," said the firstborn son. "What right does Truth-Holder to tell us what to do?"

"He made you."

"He loves you."

"He wants the very best for you."

"I will do whatever I wish," said the son.

The groom held his bride close; the bride wrapped her arms around his heart. Whatever she wanted, he would give.

"All I wish," she whispered in his ear, "is for your people to commit their lives to the rider of the clouds who holds lightning in his hands."

"Then it shall be," he promised.

The Northern Kingdom was now stronger than it had ever been. The dynasty of the castle was respected throughout the hills and valleys and deserts of the Blue Planet. The once humble king became fierce and proud as he slept soundly in his impregnable citadel. But late one night, when the lamps burned low, the angel of death walked into the royal bedchamber and took the king's breath. The kingdom mourned for many days.

The second king of the castle expanded the beautiful city. He built a splendid two-story palace with a peaceful central courtyard of shallow pools and stately palms and fragrant flowers. The walls of the building were inlaid with so much ivory that the people called it the ivory palace.

To make his demanding queen happy, the king built a majestic temple next to his ivory palace. He brought the two golden calves to the temple and set them side by side. Then he had the finest craftsmen make a golden statue that stood upon the backs of the calves. On his head were the horns of a bull. In his right hand was a blazing bolt of lightning, in his left was a weapon of war. All the people of the city came to the temple and offered spotless, new-born lambs to the rider of the clouds.

The one beyond the sky was angered at what he saw and stirred the king of the City of Caravans against the Northern Kingdom. The Caravan King mustered his army and was joined by other kings and rulers, whose realms reached across the Fertile Crescent. Thousands of horsemen and chariots and foot soldiers besieged the city on the hill.

"My citadel is impregnable," shouted the Castle King to those who surrounded his city.

"We shall wait beside your water supply and see," shouted back the commander of the great army.

It was true. In all his planning for the great city, the king had not thought of protecting his sources of water.

A week passed and the city grew dry.

Finally Castle King sent his ambassadors, "What do you demand?" The king of the City of Caravans gave his reply:

"I want your riches.

"I want your slaves.

"I want to destroy your beautiful city."

The elders of the city begged the king not to give in to such a demand.

Castle King sent back his reply: "You may have our riches and our slaves, but you may not have our city."

"Then every soul within your walls will soon be dust," declared the king of the City of Caravans.

Inside the city, the truth-teller stood before Castle King. "I have heard the whisper of the wind and this is what it says: 'Today you shall see victory, and you will know that I am above all.'"

"How can this be?" asked the king.

"When the sun touches the roof of the sky, send out your youngest soldiers. Truth-Holder will strengthen them and they shall defeat your enemy."

When the sun touched the roof of the sky Castle King opened his gates and sent out his youngest soldiers. It was the heat of the day, and the battlefield was empty. Scouts raced to the tent of Caravan King. The kings were all there together, celebrating the defeat of the City on the Hill and the Northern Kingdom. Their eyes were drowsy and their speech slurred.

"Men are advancing from the city!" said the scouts.

Caravan King turned to the scouts. "Tell the warriors to capture these men, whether they come in peace or war."

So the force was arranged carelessly, for there was little concern about this small force that was already hard upon them. In the heat the young warriors of the city were nearly mad to reach the sources of water, and their arms were strengthened by the one above all. They sliced through the force sent against them. By the time Caravan King saw that the threat was serious, the enemy had reached his very camp and death was all about. The great army ran for its lives, leaving most of its armor and horses behind.

That night water flowed in the city, and few thought of giving thanks to the rider of the clouds. It was Truth-Holder who received the people's praise.

The queen was most displeased.

The following day the man of truth returned to the presence of the Castle King. "The one above all has done all he promised. But beware, for the Caravan King shall return to avenge his honor."

Next spring Caravan King did return, attacking the plains where his war chariots could be used. He stormed the City on the Stream, a well-fortified settlement east of the Stormy Sea on the main road to the City on the Hill.

Castle King marched north, outnumbered once again. The mighty army of Caravan King circled the city. Caravan King waited for just the right moment—but so did Castle King.

The man of truth came to Castle King by night. "Again I have heard the whisper of the wind. These are the words of Truth-Holder: 'Tomorrow you shall attack, and you will see victory. Once again all will know that I am higher and greater and stronger than the rider of the clouds. But you must show no mercy to any, from the king to his armorbearers. If you fail to obey in this it will be your downfall.' "

The next morning, as the sun touched the Mountains of the Dawn, the rams' horns blew. So long had the Caravan King's army waited that the impatient horsemen and chariots did not follow their plan. Some got in the way of others, and confusion gave way to panic as Castle King hammered their weakest point. The charge split the forces of the City of Caravans, so Castle

King could meet groups of his enemy one at a time instead of all together.

The invading army was utterly destroyed.

Caravan King and a remnant fled back toward the City on the Stream. Farmers and merchants from miles around had gathered there, an untrained band of citizens who had pledged themselves to stand against this threat. When the Caravan King reached the gate of the City on the Stream and crowded its walls, weapons of all sorts rained death down from high above. The defenders used levers to topple the very stones of their own walls to crush the army below. Of the horde that had set out, not many warriors returned to the City of Caravans. The mourning of that land was great.

But Caravan King and some of his officers stripped off their armor and hid their swords and mingled with the victorious citizens. They found an unused storehouse in which to hide.

"We are doomed," said the officers to the king. "Our only hope is to humble ourselves."

When the victorious Castle King reached the City on the Stream ragged men ran through the city gate to stand before his war chariot. With torn clothing and bowed heads they fell before Castle King. "If you let us return to our homes, I will give you wealth and cities and trading rights throughout my lands," said the defeated king.

Such wealth spoke louder than the words of Truth-Holder. Castle King gave the humbled invaders safe passage and an escort to their city.

For three springs there was peace between Castle King and Caravan King. During this pause the Northern and Southern Kingdoms joined forces in an alliance. The daughter of the evil queen of the North was sent to the City of Palms in the South, where she wed the king's son. One day she would be the Wicked Queen of the Southern Kingdom. But for now all the People of the Promise celebrated their new alliance with their kinsmen.

The following spring, Caravan King gathered a new army. Once more he invaded.

Castle King called.

Sailor King came.

Together they plotted war.

Castle King brought four hundred keepers of his magnificent temple to the banquet hall. "Shall we go to the City of Refuge and battle Caravan

King or shall we stand back?" he asked them.

Shining One whispered in their ears. "Go, and you shall have victory."

Across the Winding River traveled the Army of the North and the Army of the South. The City of Refuge was in the hands of Caravan King. There they engaged in battle. In the midst of the fighting, a single shaft found its target in Castle King's body. His head spun as blood soaked his clothes.

"I've been wounded," he gasped. "Get me into a chariot and get me out of the fighting."

For the remainder of the day, Castle King sat watching the ebb and flow of war. As the sun sent out its last light, his vision flickered and was dark.

The king was laid beside his father in the beautiful city the two had built. The queen went to the temple and bowed before the rider of the clouds who stood upon the golden calves.

"Why have you betrayed me?" she wailed. "Your keepers promised victory, but now our king has fallen. Where is the victory?"

The one with lightning in his hands was silent. Even the ancient snake, coiled in the corner, made no reply.

The queen found no victory.

She felt no comfort in her grief.

She saw no hope for the future.

TO IGNORE THE MAKER OF RAIN
BRINGS MANY DRY DAYS
AND EMPTY YEARS.

CHAPTER 4

THE LISTENER

In the early days of Castle King, there lived a teller of truth who knew Truth-Holder like a son knows his father. He was lean and muscular, with a weathered face. His beard grew long and tangled. His clothes were coarse and his sandals worn. He walked with indifference to life, because his eyes looked beyond the dark images of the Blue Planet.

He lived without wife or children in the desolate hill country east of the Winding River. He was a simple man with a tender heart and a keen ear for the words of Truth-Holder. As a small child his father told him the stories of those who listened to the wind. As a young man he had learned to read the ancient scrolls in the sanctuary of the City of Palms. He buried each word deep in his soul. As the sun brightened the Mountains of the Dawn, he walked with his maker.

They talked.

They laughed.

They shared their hearts.

And he listened, for he loved the strength and purity and sweetness of the voice of Truth-Holder. The Listener was filled with joy. How could one be more happy than to walk each morning with the infinite and eternal and all-powerful? On one such walk, when a brisk wind of cold weather blew through the rocks, he heard the words of Truth-Holder.

"My wish is for you to go to Castle King!"

"What shall I say?"

"Long ago I told General that if my children bowed before Shining One, I would bring famine upon them. Castle King has set a golden man upon two golden calves. His wicked wife orders all to bow before this worthless form. Now is the time for famine."

The ground was already dry and dusty and thirsty. The rainy season was late. Worried farmers studied the cloudless sky. They sacrificed to the statue in the temple.

The rugged man with coarse clothes walked through the gates of the City on the Hill and past the guards and into the ivory palace. No one noticed his presence until he stepped through the curtains into the very audience room of Castle King. He interrupted the proceedings to say the words that had been given to him.

"I am called Listener, because I listen to the one who rules the sky. He has decreed that there will be neither rain nor dew until the people acknowledge the one who is above all."

The king stared silently at this rough-looking stranger in anger and fear.

The queen faced the truth-teller, her eyes ablaze.

"I have killed all who speak the words of Truth-Holder. The rider of the clouds rules the rain.

"Can Truth-Holder hold back the lightning?

"Can he control the sky?

"Can he keep me from killing you this day?"

"Truth-Holder can and will do whatever he wishes," said Listener.

"Kill him!" screamed the queen.

But where was he? He had already left the audience chamber. He was nowhere about the palace, and a thorough search of the city did not even find anyone who recalled seeing this unusual man. As the sun set and lamps were lit, the queen paced the ramparts of the citadel. She listened to the hiss of a serpent.

"This man is very dangerous," said the ancient one.

"He slipped through the gates, but I will search out this traitor. After he is bound and beaten, we shall see how bold he is. When he bows before the rider of the clouds, I might spare his life."

"Beware, my queen. Truth-tellers such as Listener are not easy to kill."

Listener was unmoved by the queen's searchers. He kept his face skyward in his hiding place and waited for night.

"What shall I do?" he asked the wind.

"Cross the Winding River to the place called Lonely Creek. Castle Queen will not find you there. I will be with you. I will meet your every need."

So with a full moon as his light, Listener turned toward the river. After two days' journey he stepped into a deep, desolate ravine and drank from the rippling waters of Lonely Creek. Trying to hold back his hunger, he thought of the bread that Land-Giver had given in the great desert. Perhaps Truth-Holder would do the same.

Between the heat of the afternoon and the cold of the desert night, Listener was dozing when he felt something sharp dig into his skin. He awakened to find a large black bird clutching his shoulder.

"Go away!" he shouted. "I will not to be your supper this night."

The bird flapped its large wings and dropped something before flying into the cloudless sky. Listener found half a loaf of bread in his lap. The bread looked fresh-baked and felt warm to the touch. But it had been touched by a carrion bird. He would die before he ate such unclean food.

"Listener, are you not hungry?" The question reverberated off the rocks.

"Yes, my master."

"Then eat the evening meal my hands have prepared."

Now the truth-teller noticed that the rest of the loaf was on the rock beside him, dropped by a second raven that was even larger than the first. Instead of pulling back, he reached out and touched the bird. It submitted to his gentle hand.

Never had bread tasted so good, not even when it was just taken from the coals. It was wholesome and satisfying.

Every morning and evening the two ravens returned to Listener's side with fresh bread. He stroked their dark feathers and gave them names and taught them to respond at his command. The male raven and his mate were Listener's friends as cloudless days passed and the sun beat hard upon a desolate land.

The plants died.

The animals suffered.

Lonely Creek shriveled to a dry streambed.

Listener had but a single skin of water left when the wind spoke again.

"Go east," said the wind, "past the City on the Hill to the land of the Coastal King, to a widow working at the gate of a small village."

Listener stood and started his journey without hesitation. Days later he stood at the gate of the village, hungry and thirsty and exhausted. He had passed many processions taking the dead to their graves. Fishermen caught few fish along the shores of the Great Sea. Farmers had lost all hope. Gloom was everywhere.

The truth-teller watched a small, bent woman in a thin tunic gather sticks in an ancient grove of gnarled oaks. She was not old, but her eyes were hollow and dull and lifeless. Slowly, almost painfully, she walked toward the gate.

"I am a visitor to your village," said Listener. "May I have a drink of water to quench my thirst?"

"Sir, you have the look of one who knows Truth-Holder."

"He has blessed me with his presence, and I stand here at his command."

The woman lowered her eyes.

"You are a truth-teller. I have never met one, but I see it in your face. I would be honored to give you a drink." The woman quickened her step to meet his request.

"May I also have a piece of bread to eat?"

The woman stopped at these words and burst into tears.

"I have only a handful of flour and a few drops of oil, enough for one more loaf. I am a widow, and my son is sickly. We are starving. I am gathering these sticks to make a small fire for our final meal. Tonight my son and I will eat. Tomorrow he will die, and I shall follow closely."

"Dear woman," said Listener, "if you have the faith to share your last loaf with me, then you and your son will eat many more meals. Go home and make your fire. Knead your flour and oil into two small loaves. Bring one to me and split the other with your son. After this day your bowl of flour will not be empty nor your jar of oil run dry until the famine breaks."

The widow wiped away her tears and looked at the man.

"It is a small thing for the hopeless to act in desperation. But I have tried to follow Truth-Holder though my husband died and my little one has grown weak. I will do as you say, and I will try to do it in confidence and not desperation."

The truth-teller nodded in understanding.

The two loaves were made, but there was still a little more oil and a little more flour. In fact when she had given the loaf to the stranger and shared the other with her son, there seemed quite enough of both for another loaf. And by the next morning there certainly was flour for two full loaves. The earthen jar had enough oil inside that she could feel it slosh back and forth.

She dared to hope. She made her daily bread, and there seemed not less, but more. She began to spend time each day, pushing her fingers into the full bowl of flour and letting it sift through her fingers. Not only was there enough and to spare, but it was a fine flour such as she could not grind herself. The oil was pure. There was enough that Listener anointed the head of her son so that he began to grow stronger.

Her eyes twinkled as she knelt before Listener. "You have given us more than life."

"Thank the one who lives beyond the sky."

From the first night, Listener had accepted her gift of lodging in what had been her husband's small workshop. It had been long since he had slept under a roof, and he enjoyed the lingering smell of a carpenter's tools and wood shavings.

"What shall I do now?" he asked the wind.

"Wait."

Each morning he and the widow walked together with Truth-Holder. Each day he ate fresh bread that tasted almost as good as the bread the ravens had set before him. Each day he played with the little boy. But the child continued to be pale, and sometimes to fight for breath, until one day as he tried to play in the morning sunshine he could not breathe at all. Listener was working in the small garden, trying to give just enough water to coax life into the plants. He heard the scream and found the mother cradling her child, whose breath was gone and whose heart was not beating.

"I have given all I could to Truth-Holder," she sobbed. "Why wasn't it enough?"

Listener gently lifted the boy out of her arms and carried him to his small bed. Then he cried to the one beyond the sky:

"You hold the stars in your hands. You can do all things. You can even dry a widow's tears by giving back her child's breath."

Suddenly there was a stirring.

Then a gurgling cough.

Then a fluttering of eyelids.

Listener called to the grieving mother.

"Look; your son is alive!"

The widow burst into the room, looked at the open eyes of her child and saw that color was returning to his skin. Now her tears were of joy. She squeezed her child until Listener begged her to let him rest.

Many summers later the children in the village loved to gather in the carpenter's shop. The carpenter was a huge man with several children of his own playing in the wood chips. He would do feats of strength for the children and tell them about a little boy who had nearly starved in the great famine and had, in fact, died for a while.

"But Truth-Holder just wouldn't let me stay dead," he said with a barrel laugh. "He knew your fathers would need plows and patched boats."

In the third year of the famine a breeze blew into the city and whistled in Listener's ear: "It is time. Stand before Castle King and tell him that I will send rain upon the land."

Listener said good-bye to the generous widow and her healthy son. He looked up at the cloudless skies and set out across a desolate land.

Castle King had been working to save some of his most valuable breeding horses and mules and cattle. The manager of his property searched to the north for land where some grass still grew. The king searched to the south. Now neither could find a place for the animals to graze.

On a dry, dusty road the manager met Listener. He bowed before the man with the tangled beard and coarse clothes.

"I too walk with Truth-Holder. I have heard much about you."

"I have also heard much about you," said Listener. "You have hidden many keepers of the sanctuary from Castle Queen in caves. You provide their food and water. Now do another service for the one above all. Tell your king that I wish to see him. Tell him that the time for rain and for hope and for truth has come."

WHEN TRUTH AND FALSEHOOD ARE PUT TO THE TEST, THERE CAN BE ONLY ONE WINNER.

CHAPTER 5

THE CONTEST

Listener sat in the weak shade of a sycamore that showed the stress of three years without rain. It still lived, but some forests and fields would never return to life on the parched landscape. The truth-teller watched with the hint of a smile as the king puffed along the road, surrounded by guards and servants. Castle King prided himself on his fine horses, but he would not ride one through this heat. The king was still a ways off when his first angry shouts reached Listener.

"You, you murderer of my people! Look what you have done. The kingdom is destroyed for want of rain. Look at it!"

"Why blame me for the drought? Can't the one who rides the clouds supply your cisterns?"

"You have bewitched the skies!"

"No, king. You need look no further than yourself to find the source of famine." Listener stood quietly, looking squarely and steadily and unafraid into the king's face.

"You turned your back on the one who holds stars—and clouds—in his hands. It was not enough to follow the unbelief of your fathers. You have starved the land of truth by bowing to a golden god who is nothing but a puppet for Shining One."

"Perhaps Truth-Holder has beaten back Shining One for now. But they both live beyond the sky and the rider of the clouds will win the victory."

"Put your master to the test, if you dare. Send word through your kingdom that I will stand against every prophet of the rider of the clouds. Tell them to meet me at Green Mountain. There we shall see who follows truth and who follows a lie."

"Prove to me that there is none greater than Truth-Holder and I will declare throughout my kingdom that he is the only truth. Fail and you will die. Perhaps the death of his enemy will cause Shining One to break the drought."

"It is agreed."

A throng journeyed down the Western River to where Green Mountain watched over the Great Sea. Some came because they wanted to know who was above all. Others came because it might take their minds off their troubles. Whatever happened, they could tell their children's children that they had been on the mountain to see the historic match of power. Whoever won, it would be a good story.

So the plateau at the base of Green Mountain was filled. The mountain was no longer green but brown and barren. So was the valley beside it. Onlookers noticed that someone had thought to bring many jars of water. Perhaps they could have a drink later.

The event began with fanfare. A stately parade of richly dressed keepers of the evil temple slowly marched up the path, to the sound of horns and drums and cymbals. There were four hundred and fifty keepers, their faces marked with the tattoos of those who were holy to the one who rode the clouds. Castle King and his servants and courtiers followed the keepers.

The contender stood alone in the early morning shadows. Listener had spent the night alone on the mountain, walking with Truth-Holder.

"Begin!" ordered the king.

Listener stood on a rock and shouted: "People of the Northern Kingdom. You have spent your energy following anything that comes along. Make up your minds. Whose side are you on? We are here to find the truth. Once you have seen it, follow it."

Listener looked at the opposition. "Four hundred and fifty to one," he taunted. "Are there enough of you to stand before the one who is infinite and eternal and all-powerful? Sacrifice your offering to the rider of the clouds, but do not light it with your own fire. We shall see who answers with fire from above."

The keepers looked at one another in concern, then took stones and built an altar. They choose a bull and cut its throat. When its struggles had stilled they placed it upon the stone altar. Then they called upon their golden god to burn their sacrifice with fire. They cried out to the rider of the clouds who holds lightning in his hands.

"Come to us.

"Show us your power.

"Answer our cry."

There was no response, so they shouted louder. They raised their hands and danced about and begged for a bolt of lightning. This went on for hours until they were exhausted, and the people watching were quite tired of it all. They tried to find shade in which to eat the food they had brought and to drink from their skins. Some looked longingly at all the jars of water.

As the sun touched the top of the sky Listener called out: "Shout louder. It is hot today. He may be drowsy."

The keepers danced with new purpose, wildly slashing at their arms with knives. Their fine clothes were streaked with blood. All afternoon the four hundred and fifty called, but their sacrifice remained untouched.

"The test is unfair," said a quiet voice in the minds of those who were watching. "Kill the truth-teller and go home."

But no one paid any attention to the voice of Shining One.

Finally Listener stood and faced the people.

"It is enough! Look to me."

Strong servants helped him build a pile of rock for an altar. Then he cut the throat of a young bull and set it upon his altar. Now the men followed his instructions by digging a trench around the altar. Tired as they were, the people were also curious.

"Bring water. Pour it over the sacrifice."

Servants wrestled four large jars and poured them over the bull.

"Do it again."

They did.

"Do it once more."

Thirsty onlookers could hardly stand to watch the water run off the altar and overflow the trenches. Listener stepped forward and raised his hands and looked beyond the sky.

"These people do not know you. Let them see who you are so they will long for hearts that hear your voice."

A strong wind whipped around the altar. The mountain shook. Thunder echoed from a cloudless sky. Terror gripped the hearts of the people and the keepers and the king, but they did not move. Far away in the infinite blue a spark of light grew into a ball of flame that rushed toward them. It struck the altar with the sound of a thousand lightning bolts crashing into the mountain.

All was still. The fire was gone. The people looked at where the sacrifice had been and stirred. Before them was a hole in the ground.

The bull was consumed.

The stones of the altar were gone.

The wet earth had burned away to the underlying rock.

The people fell to the ground, covering their faces. "Truth-Holder is above all," they cried out.

"Higher than the rider of the clouds.

"Higher than the golden calves.

"Higher than Shining One."

"Seize the four hundred and fifty who taught the lie and led you to ruin!" exclaimed Listener. "Let none escape."

So defeated were the keepers of Shining One's temple that they meekly walked down the path into the Valley of Harvest, toward their deaths. To the moment when they were killed they refused to look beyond the sky, for Shining One steeled each heart to face the blade.

The wind whispered to Listener, "Now the people know I am the one of consuming fire. I will show them that I am the one who sends rain as well. Far to the west a storm is stirring."

Listener went to Castle King.

"It is time to celebrate the coming of rain and the end of famine."

In the distance a small white cloud rose from the sea. As it came closer, it grew large and black and full of fury.

Castle King felt the rising wind. He drove his chariot toward the City of Harvest, where his queen waited for news of the death of Listener. The horses tossed their heads in fierce joy, as cool water flowed over their graceful bodies. They kicked away to a full gallop. The king could not see the road before him in the downpour. In the valley behind him a great dance had broken out, thousands of revelers lifting their faces to the drenching water and holding up their rain-streaked hands.

The darkly clouded sky was darker still as Castle King entered the gates of the city.

Waiting for him stood Listener.

"How is it that you are already here?"

"My legs have the strength of Truth-Holder. I come to see you keep your word. You have said that you would announce that Truth-Holder is above all."

That thought seemed distasteful to the king, but not so distasteful as telling the queen that her four hundred and fifty temple keepers had been executed. She was enraged beyond even his expectations.

She threw her crown against the wall.

She beat her husband to the floor.

She screamed obscenities at the sky.

Servants scattered. She demanded that the king send a message throughout the kingdom—a message that whoever delivered Listener's head into her hands would be richly rewarded.

News of her words awakened Listener from a peaceful sleep. The king's manager helped him slip out the gates with food for his travels from the queen's table. He ran for three days to the southernmost point of the Southern Kingdom.

Finally he could run no longer and collapsed beneath the meager shade of a stunted broom tree, wondering to himself why he had faced the fierce temple keepers but fled the anger of one evil queen.

"Let the queen kill me. I have failed. The Northern Kingdom will never know the truth," he said with wrenching sobs. Suddenly a glowing figure towered over him—

with a compassionate face

and comforting words

and a gentle touch.

A flat table stone nearby had been set with a loaf of warm bread and a jar of sweet water. Listener drank deeply and ate as one starved. Then he slept through the day and into the star-streaked night.

The brilliant figure returned with more bread and water. He touched Listener and spoke softly, "Get up and eat, for today you begin a journey."

He traveled through the scrub brush wilderness forty nights, until he reached the craggy mountain where General had received the Ten Words so long ago. There he went into a cave and built a fire.

A wind howled through the cave.

"Why are you here?"

"Castle Queen hates you and is trying to kill me. I have failed."

"You have not failed, for the victory was never up to you. I am still above all, even if no one acknowledges me. Go outside your cave and I will show you."

A great storm tore across the craggy mountain, whipping up dust and ripping at anything in its path.

Suddenly the earth shook, knocking Listener from his feet. Rocks crashed down the mountain in a thunderous avalanche of destruction.

Then the sky broke open with blinding-white fire that struck the mountain above Listener's head. Glowing sparks fell like a thousand stars around him.

Listener got to his feet. All seemed calm. A barely audible sound came from somewhere far away. Was it his imagination? He was sure he had heard something.

There it was again—a soft, distinct whisper.

"You have seen a terrible storm and a quaking of the earth and a fire from on high. These are great and powerful forces, but was I in them?"

"You sent them, but you were not in them."

"Then am I not to be found?"

"No, you are in the voice that whispers soft and still in the night."

The voice paused to let that new reality sink in. Then it began again, louder this time.

"One more task you have. Go back to where you began. There you will find another. Anoint his head with oil and help him learn to speak my words as you have."

The next day Listener set out down the craggy mountain, back toward where he had begun, back to where another would take his place and begin anew.

A LIFE LEAVES A SHADOW
OF DISGRACE OR LOVE.
FUTURE GENERATIONS WALK
IN THAT SHADOW.

CHAPTER 6

THE TWO SONS

Castle King had seventy sons, all of whom clung to the god who had failed to send fire in the great contest. When the king was killed at the City of Refuge, the crown was given to his firstborn son. But the new king fell from a high window of the ivory palace.

Bones were broken.

Flesh was torn.

There were deep injuries.

Servants carried him into the palace. Healers surrounded him. Castle Queen comforted him.

"There is a city in the western lowlands," said his mother. "They worship the silver fly that can heal any wound, no matter how serious." So the king sent runners to the lowlands to the silver fly.

Along the road through the highlands a man with rough clothing and a wild beard blocked their path.

"The king has sent you for healing to the silver fly. Go back. Ask him why he has not turned for help to the one who first breathed life into man? Since he has not, he will never leave his bed."

How did this stranger know of their mission? How could he speak with such authority? Could his words be true? After much discussion the runners obeyed the stranger and returned to the city.

The king was weak and pale, but he pushed himself up with great effort when they gave the message.

"What sort of man gave you these words?"

"A man of coarse clothes and a long, tangled beard."

"It is the man of magic. My mother has sworn to destroy him," said the king in fear. "His charms keep me in this bed."

He sent warriors to capture Listener. They found him sitting atop a small hill beneath an ancient, twisted fig tree.

"You are commanded to come down by the name of the king and the rider of the clouds," shouted the captain.

"By the name of Truth-Holder, may fire fall upon you as in the great contest. Then the king will know," said Listener.

Fire flamed from above, consuming the captain and his men.

Now the king was more determined to capture this man who mocked his power. He sent another company.

The captain found the truth-teller waiting under the fig tree. "If Truth-Holder is truly greater than the rider of the clouds, come down."

"If Truth-Holder is greater than the rider of the clouds, fire will flash from the sky," said Listener.

Again fire flamed from above, and the soldiers perished.

In fury the dying king sent out a third captain with his company. When the captain saw Listener he set down his sword and climbed the slope and bowed low.

"Have mercy on me and my loyal men. I know Truth-Holder is above all."

"Do not be afraid," said the old truth-teller. He stood and led the captain down the hillside.

When Listener and the warriors moved through the city, the streets were lined with hundreds of curious onlookers. He did not look like a prisoner. Confident and unafraid, Listener walked unbound as though he commanded the company of men who followed with their sharp swords. The rugged man awed all who stood about the bedchamber when he entered the room to face the pale king. Though in great pain, the monarch had marshaled his strength to face his enemy.

"Only the touch of the one beyond the sky can heal you, but you and your mother refuse to turn to him. Your dynasty will be cut off."

The king lifted a shaky finger to Listener. "Even if I die, the castle dynasty will never fade."

"Every son of your father will be destroyed," said Listener boldly. "And wild dogs will fight over the body of your mother."

"My mother is a noble woman. . ." The king coughed deep in his chest.

He paused for a gasp of breath before pronouncing doom on this man. His mouth moved, but no sound came forth. His eyes glazed over, and a serpent sighed.

Healers and servants and aids rushed to the bed but could do nothing. Listener left the room and the ivory palace and the city without being stopped. He shook his head.

"If only he had cried out to Truth-Holder."

At the Place of the Portal, Listener met Seer.

They spoke of the greatness of Truth-Holder.

They reminisced about the life of Listener.

They talked of his departure from the Blue Planet.

One afternoon Listener said to Seer, "The one beyond the sky calls me on. I must go to the cities of the North. Stay here and wait."

"As long as you walk the Blue Planet, I will walk by your side," Seer answered.

So the two traveled the highlands together, encouraging those who clung to the one who holds stars in his hands. Days later they stood on the west bank of the Winding River. The water was high.

Listener took off his ancient coat of coarse wool weave. Seer watched as Listener rolled it around his wooden staff. He stood on the bank and struck his cloak on the water with all his strength.

"Whoosh."

Ripples moved outward, growing into a great wave. The wave pushed back the water of the river.

A bed of sand and rock and flopping fish lay before them. Invisible hands held back the water. The cloak was dry when Listener unrolled it and put it on over his tunic. Then the two walked across on dry land.

"Today I shall be taken," said Listener. "What can I give you before I go?"

"All I ask is to walk in your steps," said Seer. "I ask for the faith to continue."

"You and I are but servants, and we have only what the master gives. So we will look to our master to stretch your faith."

Through the day the two walked and talked. Listener told the ancient tales of the Book of Beginnings. He told of the Garden and the Exile and Walker. Suddenly the day turned twilight. It seemed the moon had caught fire and was blazing toward them. Now Seer could see that the fiery object looked like a great golden glowing chariot, drawn by flaming stallions. Nearly touching the ground, an angel reached out and pulled Listener aboard. In a moment the glorious chariot was gone. From its high path an object floated downward on the swirling air currents. It settled a short distance away.

Seer watched as the sky returned to its late afternoon brightness. Then he walked to the object. It was the coarse woolen cloak by which all recognized his teacher.

Seer held the coat tight. He ran his fingers across the fabric, thinking of all that Listener had done. He looked to the deepening twilight and asked for faith, but instead he felt weak and needy and dependent on Truth-Holder. He had less confidence in himself, but more in the one above all.

He walked back toward the Winding River by moonlight. Standing on the bank, he watched the angry dark waters flow by.

"Truth-Holder, I am as empty as this river is full. You filled Listener. Will you fill me?" Seer took off the cloak and wrapped it around his staff and struck the flowing water.

Ripples scattered.

The water divided.

Invisible hands held it back.

Word spread that Seer had taken the power of Listener. He was overwhelmed with unworthiness, yet those who had known Listener agreed that the spirit of the teacher now rested on the student. Slowly Seer grew into what Truth-Holder had made of him.

The secondborn son of Castle King was crowned ruler of the Northern Kingdom in his dead brother's place. The new king was no different, however, in following the ways of his mother and Shining One.

Many springs before, the defeated People of the Plains had made peace with Castle King. Now they refused to pay the tribute due. So the kingdom army was raised and runners were sent south to the Sailor King.

"Come with me to fight the People of the Plains," the message urged.

"My people are your people," said Sailor King.

The armies joined and marched south to the Salty Sea and then turned toward the rising sun. They traveled light through the barren wilderness, hoping to surprise the People of the Plains. But their supplies ran low.

"All our warriors and strategies are for nothing," cried the Northern

King. "We will either die of thirst or the Plains People will capture us out of pity."

"Is there no prophet of Truth-Holder with your army?" asked Sailor King.

"I have brought keepers of the one who rides the clouds," the Northern King replied. "Those who follow Truth-Holder have no place with this army."

"That is not quite true," answered one who was listening. "Along the way a young truth-teller who wears a coarse coat joined our column. He seemed to belong, so none questioned him."

"Find him," said Sailor King.

Seer was standing near the entrance to the tent. He entered and took the counselor's place before the surprised kings.

"If you seek the one beyond the sky, he will answer," he said without introduction.

"We seek Truth-Holder," said the Southern King.

"Then have your warriors dig ditches. In the morning drink deeply and overthrow the Army of the People of the Plains."

Ditches were dug.

Night fell.

In the morning every ditch was full.

The Army of the Plains People knew of their enemy's coming and was waiting in ambush on the mountain. The commanders looked down on the camp as the morning sun touched the Mountains of the Dawn with red. Reflected upon the ditches, the red sun made the valley look awash in blood.

The king of the Plains smiled. "The two kingdoms have turned against each other and fought to their deaths. The battle is ours. Now to the plunder."

The warriors of the Plains rushed into the valley, shouting loudly. When they reached the valley floor they stopped in horror. A great well-rested and well-watered army stood waiting quietly, row upon row on every side. The battle was brief. The People of the Promise celebrated, but the son of Castle King still did not look beyond the sky.

Seasons passed. The King of Caravans invaded as he had when Castle King was killed. The second son of Castle King sent runners to a new Southern King. "Will you help me avenge the death of my father?"

"Your father is my grandfather," said the new king. "I will come to avenge his death."

So the two armies joined once again and marched east to war. The kings did not understand that they marched toward the judgment of Truth-Holder.

The story of the Southern Kingdom has told of this victory against the Desert People, a victory in which the Northern King felt the bite of an enemy blade and was carried to the City of Harvest. There he was joined by the Southern King.

Thus they came to that fatal day when the commander of the northern army, offended by a thousand injustices and encouraged by ambition, cut down both kings.

The commander turned to one of his officers, "Take the king's body and throw it in an empty field. Let the ravens do to him as his evil family has done to the Northern Kingdom."

He rode his chariot on into the City of Harvest. Castle Queen had been warned. Proudly she looked at her reflection once more in a polished brass mirror.

Her tired eyes were painted.

Her thinning hair was stylishly braided.

Her tongue was still sharp.

"Deceitful traitor!" she screamed from the second-story window in the summer palace. "Have you the blood of your king on your hands?"

"Your son is dead," the commander replied.

"I have other sons to avenge his death."

"And I have many at my side to see that there will never be another Castle King."

The palace windows were crowded with the servants and officials of the kingdom.

The commander called to them: "The castle dynasty is no more. Will you stand with this shadow queen or accept the vengeance that has come upon her?"

There were screams as the servants lifted Castle Queen and heaved her from the window. The horses of the commander's men silenced her cries of rage and terror forever.

The men went into the palace to eat and drink and greeted those who had attended the king's family.

"The queen's body is lying in the street," remarked an officer.

"We will put her body in the tomb of her ancestors," said the commander.

But it was too late. Before men went out to carry away the body, the wild dogs of the city had fought over her remains.

Some remembered the words of Listener.

The dynasty of the castle was over and the commander of the army inaugurated the dynasty of the sword.

CHAPTER 7

THE SEER'S POWER

The queen who breathed death on all followers of Truth-Holder was dead. One hundred who had been hidden for years in secret limestone caves could walk about unafraid. They could again teach the Northern Kingdom the words of Truth-Holder. And they looked for leadership to Seer, the man who wore the cloak of Listener.

Seer missed the fellowship and wise words of his teacher. Why had the one beyond the sky taken Listener so soon?

Seer stood on the west side of the river and looked up. "Give me the power to do what you wish me to do."

"Humble your heart," said the wind, "and you shall do what is impossible except at my hand."

So the lean, tall man with keen eyes met with the one hundred. It was a day of deep sadness, not only for the loss of Listener, but also for the death of one of their leaders. His family had been impoverished by the years of hiding, and now his wife was a forsaken widow.

"My husband clung to Truth-Holder, but he borrowed much and was deeply in debt. Now strong men demand payment or they will take my two sons as slaves."

"What do you have in your house that might be of value?" asked Seer.

"I have only a small jar of oil."

"Go to your neighbors and gather all their empty jars. Take them to your house and fill every one of them with oil from your jar."

"How can such a thing happen?" wondered the widow.

"Truth-Holder has never let impossibilities keep him from doing all that he wanted."

So the widow collected many jars and answered vaguely when her neighbors asked why she needed them. Soon one could hardly walk across her tiny dwelling. She picked up her jar of olive oil and looked at it, then down at the dozens of large and small earthen vessels.

There were yawning wide-mouthed vats.

There were narrow-necked water jugs.

There were bowls and cups and flasks.

So she shrugged and began pouring into a bowl. It filled and still there was a little more, so she moved to a slightly larger container. It also filled, and she seemed to have just a little more.

By the end of the day she was tired from pouring. Every container was brimming with the finest olive oil, as much as a healthy grove of trees might yield in an entire season.

When every jar was filled she asked her sons to bring more.

"We have been everywhere. There are none left."

Then she noticed that only a few drips were clinging to the lip of her small jar. It was empty at last. Carefully the widow and her sons lifted bowls and carried them to the merchant who bought from the olive growers. He tasted it suspiciously, wondering how this woman had come upon so much.

"This is of a very good quality. I will be glad to buy it from you."

"Would you like more?"

"However much you have like this, I will buy."

The widow and her sons exchanged glances, thinking of the dozens and dozens of containers still crowding their house.

"We have more," they said with a laugh.

Seer traveled between the City of Palms and the City of Harvest. One day he stopped at a small town. A wealthy woman invited the traveler to share a meal and have a night's lodging. With the woman and her husband, Seer ate a hearty meal and drank fine wine and spoke of the marvels of the one above all. They became such friends that Seer visited often. So they built a small room that would always be his.

Seer was humbled by their graciousness. "How can I show my love to you both?"

The woman's face clouded. "There is only one thing we want, but that is something no one can give."

"You want a child."

She looked up in surprise that he knew this hidden ache of her heart.

"I will never have a son, for I am barren and my husband is old."

Seer placed his arm around her shoulders.

"Truth-Holder knows your dream."

When next he came to his friends, he noticed a secret smile on the face of the woman. She said nothing for a time, but she could no longer keep still.

"Today I will tell my husband a secret. Truth-Holder has placed a growing life within me."

"I know. So does your husband, for your face of love and joy has given away your secret. That is how it is with those blessed by the one above all."

In due time she held her special gift from Truth-Holder to her breast. Her son grew tall and strong and healthy—Truth-Holder's priceless gift.

A handful of summers passed. One morning as father and son worked in the barley fields, the son gave a sudden scream of pain and dropped to the ground. "My head! My head!"

His face was scarlet.

Hot tears scorched his cheeks.

His brow wrinkled with pain.

The father gently lifted his son and cringed as the cries of pain increased. When the child was placed in his mother's arms, the child grew silent and the face relaxed and the eyes closed. The mother took him into Seer's room and laid him on the bed. Then she saddled a donkey and set out for Green Mountain, where Seer was telling the people the ancient stories of Truth-Holder.

She reached the mountain meadow and rushed to Seer and fell at his feet. Seer touched his dear friend. "What has brought you such pain?"

"Truth-Holder has taken away my son."

Seer rushed to the house and knelt before the breathless boy and cried out to Truth-Holder, "Please return life to this child." Seer pressed his body against the young man. Slowly the boy's body grew warm. Suddenly there was a sneeze, and the son opened his eyes.

The mother fell to the master's feet.

"It is not by my hand that he lives," Seer reminded her. "Truth-Holder has twice given his gift and allowed you to see the possibilities in what you thought impossible."

She looked beyond the sky.

The one above all knew her heart.

Her life was never the same.

For a different reason, life was not the same for a valiant warrior who lived in the City of Caravans. He commanded the city's army. Some said he had shot the fatal arrow into Castle King in that great battle. If so, he said nothing of it.

But he was a loyal soldier and richly rewarded by the king. He was highly regarded as a man of kindness and integrity and fairness. His was a life of good fortune until the bright spot appeared on the back of his hand. As it spread and turned the skin white there was little doubt of its cause. The soldier had the most dreaded of all diseases. Those who carried this disease were despised and feared and could not come near others.

Healers came to the commander's house, but each said nothing could heal the growing spot. Soon it would spread over his body. The commander faced his future with dignity. But his wife wept at the curse. Her servant girl stayed at her side, comforting her.

In one of her deepest moments of sorrow, the wife cried out: "Is there not even one beyond the sky who will take pity on this good man?"

"Mistress," said the servant girl respectfully, "I believe there is."

The woman turned toward to her. "Is there one who can save my husband?"

"When I was a very small child, my father was killed by the evil queen of the Northern Kingdom. My mother and I were sold into slavery, and that is how I came into your service. My father died because he walked with the one who holds the stars in his hands.

"I know," she continued, "of a man with the power of Truth-Holder. Seer has great gifts of healing, and some who go to him are as hopeless as is my master."

The commander almost dared hope. But this man cared for the People of the Promise, not their enemies in the City of Caravans.

"It is useless," he said at last. "Whatever his powers, he will not help me."

"I think you will find that the man called Seer and the one he serves are less interested in one's place of birth than in hearts willing to follow. What will you lose by trying?"

The king encouraged his commander.

"I will send a letter to the ruler of the Northern Kingdom," said the Caravan King, "asking that you might see this Seer to heal your disease."

The commander loaded donkeys and horses and camels with much silver and gold. Then he rode eight days south to the capital of the Northern Kingdom.

When the king was told that a fierce chieftain of the Caravan City stood outside his gate, he sent a company of warriors out to him.

"Do you come in peace?" asked the warriors.

"Yes, and in great need," said the commander. "I have a letter from my king."

"Follow us," said the warriors.

"By your laws I cannot come into the city," said the commander, pulling back his cloak to show his arms. The warriors stepped back.

"I only ask permission to go to the one who is able to take away my sickness."

The king was troubled. He looked to his advisors. "No one can heal such a disease. He will go home and tell his king that we did not help him, and his king will attack us again."

"Maybe he believes there is a man of great power, perhaps a keeper of the one who rides the clouds."

"I know of none," said the king. "But tell the commander that he has my permission to go to anyone who can help him."

The commander turned toward the village to which his servant girl had directed him.

There the small caravan encountered a man.

"We seek the dwelling of Seer."

"I am his servant. Come with me."

The great commander stopped his chariot in front of the dwelling of Seer and put on his richest clothing to impress the truth-teller. Servants followed with his animals laden with riches. The prophet's servant returned in a few minutes.

"Seer instructs you to wash yourself seven times in the Winding River. Do that and you will be healed." The servant went back into the house and closed the door. The commander looked after him in wonder and rage and embarrassment.

"I have come with great power.

"I have brought fine riches.

"I have traveled many miles.

"How dare he not even come to the door? Instead he wants me to wash in the Winding River?"

He turned from the door and stepped into his chariot and sped from the city. That night his servants approached him. "Excuse me, exalted master," said one. "You have come so many miles, and the power of this one called Seer is your only hope. If Seer told you to fight a great and terrible beast in the Mountains of the Dawn, would you have done it?"

"Yes; I would gladly wage battle against impossible odds."

"If he had asked you to go through the desert to the Land of Pyramids and steal a jewel, would you have done it?"

"We would be on our way," he admitted.

"Then why not do this? The servant girl said this one above the sky cares for nothing except a heart willing to follow."

The commander considered these words. In the morning he turned toward the Winding River. He stripped off his fine clothes and entered the dirty water and scrubbed at his diseased skin. He did it again and again and again. Six times he came out feeling that he was being made to look a fool.

Nonetheless, he went into the water a seventh time and washed. This time his skin began to tingle and sting and peel. Even the pain felt refreshing. He came up out of the water and touched the places of his most hideous blisters. They were gone. He ran his fingers over his neck and chest. There was no trace of swelling. He stared at his hand. It was tan and healthy.

He shouted out in joy, and all who were with him joined in his happiness. He ran back to the city and pounded on Seer's door.

"I am healed! I am healed!" he shouted in ecstasy. A table was spread for the commander and his men, and Seer spoke with them about Truth-Holder.

"You are right that none is so powerful," the commander said. "No one can contend with Truth-Holder. Now take my silver and gold. Do with it whatever you wish. Build some great temple or live in luxury, for you have given me life."

"It is Truth-Holder who has healed you. He does not require your gold."

"Will you take no silver or gold?"

"I want none of it. If you wish to thank me and thank Truth-Holder, then follow his ways. Your servant girl can tell you how."

The commander bowed low. "I shall never forget this day or the Winding River or the one who washed away the most dreaded of diseases."

The prophet touched his shoulder and said, "Go in peace."

WHAT WE SEE SAYS MORE ABOUT US THAN IT SAYS ABOUT WHAT CAN BE SEEN.

CHAPTER 8

THE SEER'S VISION

When blossoms colored the trees pink and white, the king of the City of Caravans ordered the commander to take the army into the Northern Kingdom. The commander knew he risked his life to go against the king, but he was ordered to take war to the country of Seer. The one above all had washed away the curse from his body at the word of Seer.

"But this is the season of war," said the king. He had sent his dying commander to the Northern Kingdom and had seen him come back healed. He understood how his friend and servant felt.

"Please give my command to another," the man pleaded. "Seer saved my life. How can I threaten his people?" The commander did not tell the king that he also had become a follower of Truth-Holder, and felt himself a kinsman to those of the Northern Kingdom who still followed the one above all.

"You have led my army to many victories. Prepare a new commander to take your place," said the king.

A new commander was chosen.

Battles were plotted.

Armies secretly marched into position.

A wind blew through the streets of the City of Sight, a town on a hill about half a day's journey north of the ivory palace. The wind found Seer and told him of the coming attack and where it would come. The Northern Army was sent to wait for the invaders. Only the sharp eyes of the Caravan Army's scouts saved them from a disaster.

"They knew we were coming, and where," complained the king to his advisors.

"Could your former commander have told them?" said one advisor, who had long been jealous of the wealth and influence of the army commander. Caravan King, however, had already considered this.

"He knew that the attack was planned, but not its route. That information could only have come from someone among us," the king said.

So the king repositioned his army to cross into the Northern Kingdom at a remote place. But no sooner had he crossed than he found a vastly superior army was again waiting for him. No matter where he positioned his troops, the Northern King was prepared.

"Someone betrays me."

"None of us," said the advisors with some fear. "We have learned that your plans are told by Seer, the man who healed your commander. He seems to know all you say and do."

"Find him," shouted the enraged king. "He will tell us how he learns our secrets, and he will suffer for telling them."

Spies crossed the border and spread through the countryside. They searched every valley and mountain and waterway until they learned that Seer was in the City of Sight. A large force was sent by circuitous ways to capture him

with fast horses

and armored chariots

and mighty men with swords.

In the silence of a shadowless night they reached and circled the city. As the sun lit the Mountains of Dawn, they closed in on their target.

Seer's servant rose early in the morning and stepped from his house. Looking over the valley, his heart trembled in fear. "Oh, my master," he called. "Come and see. The enemy is upon us."

"Yes, I know," said Seer, and he calmly came to his servant's side and looked at the mighty force in the hills surrounding the town. "Do not be afraid," he said. "Our army is greater than theirs."

"But the army is miles from here."

"Swords will protect us," said Seer.

"We have no swords. We have no defenses. We have nothing."

Seer looked beyond the sky. "Truth-Holder, open his eyes."

The servant suddenly saw with new vision. The world before him was brighter and clearer and more real than he had ever seen. And between the city where he stood and the oncoming army were a thousand shining angels. Each clutched a flaming sword and rode a golden chariot pulled by a pair of horses that glowed brighter than the sun.

"I see," said the servant. "I truly see."

A signal was given, and the enemy army moved down toward the city. When the warriors of the Caravan King raced headlong into their unseen enemy, Truth-Holder struck each soldier with blindness.

Horses' reins were pulled.

Chariots abruptly stopped.

Mighty men stood lost and confused.

Seer walked toward the commander of the milling horsemen. "Why have you come to this city?" he asked.

"We have come to capture Seer," said the confused leader.

"This is not the city where you should be," said Seer. "Call your men to the road and they will see well enough to ride on. Then follow me and I will set you aright."

Seer climbed into the commander's chariot, and the warriors were summoned. As men who are drunk or wandering through a thick fog, they followed him to the royal City on the Hill. Through the gates he led them and to the steps of the ivory palace. Suddenly their eyes were opened, and their reason given back to them. And what a frightening sight they awakened to. The warriors of the Northern Kingdom stood, rank upon rank, on every side. They turned this way and that, comprehending their hopelessness but mystified as to how it had happened.

The Northern King called to Seer: "Shall I take their breath?"

"They are no danger to you," answered Seer. "Rather look upon them and learn a great lesson through their eyes: It is hard to fight against him who holds stars in his hands. Now give them food and drink and send them to their king in peace."

After this the Caravan King sent no more warriors against the Northern King for many summers. But eventually the lessons of this fruitless war were forgotten. Again Caravan King coveted the land of the Northern Kingdom. Again he readied his horses and chariots and mighty men. Soon a great army stood before the walls of the Northern Kingdom's capital. A long siege began. Silos and storage houses were emptied. People went hungry until infants and elderly died. Those who lived grew thin and weak and desperate.

The king walked through streets that were filled with tragedy. Women wept. Men sat listlessly in the shade and stared.

There were no children.

There was no laughter.

There was only the stench of death.

"Help me, oh king," cried a woman who was too weak to move.

"The only one who can save this city is Truth-Holder," answered the king. "And he does nothing."

The woman fell to the ground and wailed. "We are lost, and the king is as powerless as the poor."

"If there was anything I could do, I would do it," said the king.

"Then go to Seer and ask him what Truth-Holder wants from us. That is where we all go for help. There is no help at the ivory palace. The elders are with him now."

The king was furious. "This man undermines my throne!"

He called for the captain of the palace guard and gave his order: "Go to Seer's house and take his head. Tell the elders that Seer speaks only for Truth-Holder, and Truth-Holder has abandoned us."

Seer sat with the elders in a circle. The elders had learned to listen to the wind and walk with the one beyond the sky. Now Seer stood up and addressed his friends: "The king feels threatened by the power of the one who holds the stars in his hands. His soldiers come for my life."

"We will not let that happen," said the leaders. They secured the door against the soldiers. When he learned that the elders themselves stood against his guard, the king himself came to appeal to them. He pounded on the door. "Truth-Holder has done nothing for us," the king said. "We die, and he does not lift a finger. We weep and wail and wait, yet he is silent. Leaders of the city, open the door and follow me. If we surrender, maybe our enemy will have mercy on us and give us a crust of bread."

The leaders were tempted. One stood to open the door.

"Stop!" Seer cried. "Truth-Holder is not silent. He has waited for our humble cries to be raised. He has heard what was said in this circle and will free the city. Food will flow freely at this hour tomorrow."

The captain of the guard laughed and said, "Is flour to rain from the sky?"

Not all the suffering was in the city. Four men who suffered from the curse that disfigured their bodies stood just outside the city walls. By law they could not go through the gates into the city. And why would they want to?

"We must do something soon or we will starve," said the oldest.

"Then let us go to the camp of the enemy and beg," said a man with the disease etched deeply into his face.

"We are their enemy, and we carry the curse on our skin. They have two reasons to kill us."

"Why should they bother? We are hardly a threat. And if they kill us, they only save us from the agony of starving."

As dusk fell, the four quietly crept toward the camp. Why had no watchmen confronted them?

They walked more boldly now. The camp was in sight, so why were there no warriors? They entered a tent. It had been so long, they had forgotten what it was like to have a roof above them and walls around them. And there was raised bread and dried meat and sweet wine in plenty.

So began one of the strangest of banquets. In the heart of a great war camp, four despised men ate until their bellies could hold no more. The men were baffled at the absence of the soldiers of the camp. They kept looking for the warriors' return. But night fell, and only a few hungry jackals could be seen, enjoying themselves just as much as the four cursed men.

Only much later was it learned that the great war band had begun their evening meal, when a crash of swords and the shrill notes of rams' horns could be heard in the distance. Soldiers grabbed their weapons. The king and his guards ran from their tents. Watchmen spread the alarm that a powerful army was approaching from the south.

"How can that be?" the king asked.

"A runner must have reached the Delta and brought back a mighty force from the People of the Pyramids," said a commander. "We are not prepared to face such a foe."

Their readiness was no longer an issue, for the hearts of the entire army felt terror. Already men were mounting their horses or simply running for their lives.

So now four men sat on rich cushions in the solitude of the king's tent and wondered. They had eaten until they were stuffed. They had carried away riches. What should they do now?

"We are gorging ourselves, while people starve," said the oldest.

"You are right," said another. "Let us get a good night's sleep here on these cushions, then go tell the city the good news."

"No," said the oldest. "Let us go at once and tell our king."

So it was that soldiers were standing at the camp of their enemy before morning's light. They took horses and followed the trail of the fleeing army for a time, then raced back to the capital city.

"This is no trick," they shouted to the king at the gate. "Whatever happened, our enemies are miles away, and they have left all they possessed."

By afternoon there was more flour and barley than the people could eat, just as Seer had said. The city celebrated and praised the one beyond the sky.

But Seer bowed his head.

Sadness filled his heart.

For he knew this moment would not last.

EVIL IS CONTAGIOUS.
THE ONE WHO WOULD REMOVE IT
MAY BE THE FIRST
TO SPREAD ITS INFECTION.

CHAPTER 9

THE DYNASTY OF THE SWORD

It was a day he would never forget. That morning he had been commander of the Northern Army. Now it was evening, and he reclined with his officers around the table of the king in the summer palace in the City of Harvest. Each drank wine from a royal goblet. Those who had drunk from those goblets the night before were all dead. Now men saluted the commander with strange words.

"Long live our king. Long live his new dynasty of the sword."

Vengeance smiled at his men. "Today I sent an arrow through the heart of the Northern King. At my word the breath of the Southern King was taken. Castle Queen is no more. This is the beginning."

"The beginning of what?" asked one of his officers.

"The beginning of judgment," said Vengeance as he drank deeply from his goblet. "A full moon ago a man journeyed from the northern capital to meet me. He was a servant of Seer and he came with an important message from Truth-Holder. The servant poured a flask of clear oil over my head. The one above all had chosen me to be king over the Northern Kingdom. I am Vengeance, the sword and the destroyer. My sword destroys all that remains of the dynasty of the castle, just as they killed the followers of Truth-Holder.

"They have corrupted the land

"and followed the ways of the snake

"and rejected the words of the one beyond the sky."

Vengeance swept a sword from its scabbard and looked at it. The sword had fine and intricate and gold-inlaid carvings. It was forged of fine metal, for it had belonged to the Northern King. The new king laid it out upon the table before him.

"The servant told me to destroy every male of the house of Castle King and to put an end to the wickedness of Castle Queen. Of this we have made only a beginning."

"There remain seventy sons of Castle King," said an officer.

"And each son must face the sword," said Vengeance.

"Why has Truth-Holder chosen you?"

"Because I walk with him and listen to his words and do what he asks. The one with stars in his hands has been patient, but his patience for the Castle King and his family has been replaced by mercy for our nation. So the time has come for the sword to fall. It is the sword of Vengeance."

Those at the commander's table looked deeply into his eyes and knew that all he said was true. They stood to their feet and offered their vows. "You are our king," each declared. "We will follow you and fight for you and give our lives for you."

The next morning the commander wrote letters to the men of influence within the capital city.

"The Castle King is dead by my hand, for he was not fit to live. Justice also has taken the life of his evil mother. As soon as this letter reaches you, choose the best of his sons to take the throne. Then prepare your chariots and sharpen your swords and fortify your cities, for the Army of the North stands with me, and we are coming to destroy the wickedness that has torn our country."

The men of influence read the letter. Their hearts grew fearful.

"All of the seventy are weak and wicked," said the most respected of the men.

"Shining One has not protected us," said another.

"How can we stand against Vengeance and his entire army?" asked a third.

"It is as you say," said the most respected elder. "No one can stand against those who walk the ways of the one beyond the sky."

So the men of influence sent a reply to the commander: "We are your people. We will follow you and Truth-Holder, for none among the seventy is worthy to be king."

The commander sent his harsh instructions: "If you are on my side, come to me at the City of Harvest, carrying with you the heads of the seventy sons."

The men of influence acted quickly and silently, doing what was required of them.

They swung their swords
and slaughtered the sons
and brought to Vengeance their gift of blood.

The following morning as the people went out from the city to work their fields, Sword King stood by the gate, surrounded by the most horrible sight the people had ever seen. A stench permeated the air. Men held their breath and looked away. Children clung to their parents in fear.

All heard the words of the commander: "Truth-Holder sent me to bring judgment to the castle dynasty. So it will be." Word of what had happened went out from the city that day. All understood what would happen to those who did not follow Sword King. All the men of influence and priests of Shining One who lived in the Valley of Harvest fell to the dynasty of the sword.

Then Sword King took his sword to the capital city of the Northern Kingdom. On the road he met a large and stately caravan.

"Who are you?" he demanded.

"We are relatives of the Southern King," said the leader of the caravan. "We have traveled from the City of Palms to honor the Northern King and his seventy sons and his mother, Castle Queen."

"You are too late," said Sword King. "All you seek have been killed. Even your own king has lost his life. Today his body is being carried to the city from which you came."

"Who would do such a deed?" demanded the leader. "We are followers of Shining One. We will bow before the golden calves and the rider of the clouds and ask for retribution against the killers."

"I am the one you seek," said Sword King. "I am Vengeance and it is I who avenge the honor of Truth-Holder against the followers of Shining One."

Too late the men of the caravan saw what these words meant. They backed away as Sword King raised his weapon. "Take them to the highlands and end their lives."

Sword King continued on to the capital of the Northern Kingdom. He burst through the city gates with a fanfare of rams' horns. Word had already reached the city and warriors of the army came into the marketplace and knelt before the king.

"The day of Vengeance and the dynasty of the sword has begun," he told them. "Search out any who remain of the castle dynasty. Their lives are demanded."

Blood was spilled.

Lives were cut short.

A dynasty ended.

The days had been bathed in blood, and the people were quick to celebrate their new king, as he entered the ivory palace. Now he sat on the royal throne and set the next part of his plan into motion. Sword King stood on the steps of the ivory palace and called to the people of the city. "Justice has been restored to our country, but to whom shall we look for the future? I will follow the ways of the castle dynasty in one respect, for I have decided to follow the rider of the clouds."

Suddenly ten warriors appeared behind the crowd. Upon their muscular shoulders was the golden man standing on two golden calves, one foot planted on the back of each animal. The people stared at the statue as the warriors set it at the foot of the king.

"Let us send runners throughout the land to announce a great celebration. Let us gather all who bow before the rider. Let us stand together in a great festival at the temple of Shining One and pledge the future of our kingdom to the golden man."

Runners were sent and the festival begun. The followers filled the temple on the day of ceremony. Each received a scarlet robe to show their commitment to the rider of the clouds.

Sword King had told his warriors privately: "See that only those with scarlet robes are allowed in the temple; remove anyone who walks with the one beyond the sky."

Those within the temple bowed before the golden image and committed their hearts to darkness. As the evil smoke grew thick and confused their minds, Sword King had his warriors surround the building.

"Let no one escape," he ordered his men. "Draw your swords and break down the doors and take the breath of every person in scarlet."

Warriors slashed their way through the temple and slaughtered everyone. The bodies were thrown into the streets. The golden man who stood on the golden calves was dragged away and melted to liquid in a great fire.

The shiny pool of liquid mingled with the dirt of the street. Warriors burned all statues of the ancient snake and knocked down the supporting pillars of the temple. As the house of Shining One collapsed into rubble, the warriors spat upon the ruins and the king declared it a place of shame.

A wind blew through the capital city and swirled about Sword King. "You have done a hard thing, killing all who had polluted a very evil nation. Because you have stood as my Vengeance against the castle dynasty and destroyed those who bowed to the rider of the clouds, I am pleased. Your sons and grandsons and great-grandsons shall sit on the throne of the ivory palace. But you must follow closely or one day your family will be purged from the land."

For a time Sword King remembered the warning and walked each morning with Truth-Holder. For thirty summers he was a wise and effective ruler who took all but one step. He wanted to keep the memory of the early days of the Northern Kingdom, so he never destroyed the golden calves that had first seduced the people. In the twilight of his life his heart became weak and his eyes were drawn back to the statues.

The one beyond the sky sent warnings to Vengeance and the people. He withheld blessing. He allowed the king of the City of Caravans to press the Northern Kingdom. To the west, Caravan King claimed the coastal plain and to the east he conquered all beyond the Winding River and to the north, he pushed toward the Stormy Sea. Sword King fought valiantly. His kingdom became smaller, but it refused to fall. The boundaries were reinforced and the cities fortified and the armies ordered to stand firm.

But Sword King wore out his body in his labors and finally was taken to lie in the tomb of kings. The kingdom wept, and his oldest son was crowned.

The new king faced many trials. He was constantly besieged and embattled and threatened by the forces from the Caravan City. Besieged King fell before the golden calves and pleaded for help from Shining One and refused to hear the wisdom of Seer. So Truth-Holder increased his difficulty. His army was reduced to fifty horsemen and ten chariots and ten thousand foot soldiers. All the rest had been destroyed.

Then one day an aged man asked for an audience. Seer stood before the king with confidence and courage.

"It is not too late to see the truth and follow the one above all," said Seer.

"I am so tired of fighting against Truth-Holder. Tell me where to meet him," Besieged King responded. Seer saw and nurtured the spark of brokenness.

"Look beyond the sky.

"Walk the highlands.

"Cry out to the one who holds stars in his hands."

"If I do what you say," said Besieged King, "will we be delivered from destruction?"

"Truth-Holder will hear your cry."

Besieged King looked beyond the sky and walked the highlands and cried out to the one who holds stars in his hands. He bent his head and offered spotless, newborn lambs to the one above all.

As the sweet scent rose above the land, a new and mighty army marched across the Fertile Crescent and hammered the City of Caravans with a mighty blow. The warriors of Caravan King fled the boundaries of the Northern Kingdom and went to their city to fight off their new enemy. The Northern Kingdom rested. It was no longer besieged or embattled or threatened. The people celebrated. They thanked their king and they thanked Seer and they thanked the one beyond the sky.

Yet as summers of prosperity came, the king and his people forgot who saved them from the City of Caravans.

The king returned to the golden calves

and bowed before the statues of the snake

and reveled in the wicked ways of Shining One.

Neither king nor people realized that they were failing their final chance.

> TO BE ALMOST STRONG IS TO BE WEAK;
> TO BE WEAK AND KNOW IT,
> IS THE GREATEST STRENGTH.

CHAPTER 10

THE SAD FAREWELLS

Besieged King is dead," said the runners as they took the message throughout the kingdom.

"Who shall take the throne?" asked the leaders of the northern tribes.

"I shall," declared the king's oldest son. "Truth-Holder promised my grandfather that his family would dwell in the ivory palace for generations, and so it shall be. Let any who wish to challenge my rule, draw your sword."

No challenger stepped forward.

The claim stood.

The king was crowned.

"My father was besieged, but I shall be strong. I shall recapture all that my father and grandfather lost. The North shall again be a great kingdom and we shall make our enemies shudder."

The people cheered and Strong King went about rebuilding the Northern Army. He bought the finest horses from the Land of the Delta. He hired metal workers to build chariots. He enlisted every man of fighting age to take up their swords and bend their bows and strengthen their shields. The army now had many campfires in the hills surrounding the capital of the Northern Kingdom.

But before they went to battle, bad news arrived at the ivory palace.

"My master is very sick," said Seer's servant. "His vision is dim and his breath shallow and his legs unable to support his body."

Strong King left his palace and went to Seer's simple house on the edge of the city. He bent his head as he entered a bedchamber that could hold no more than a wooden chair and a thin mattress of straw.

Seer lay quietly, preparing to meet the one who holds stars in his hands. He was ready to rest and rejoin his teacher and walk together near the eternal house of Truth-Holder.

"Seer," said Strong King softly as he knelt on the dirt floor beside the old one's mattress. "You have been the real strength of my country. You had my grandfather anointed king and you helped my father at his point of greatest need. Let us give you our gratitude. My servants will take you to the palace. We will care for you."

"It is easy to thank an old and dying man." The words were slow and deliberate and spoken with an exhausting effort. "But from the beginning you have refused to give thanks to Truth-Holder. I am just his servant. I have walked with him and followed in the steps of Listener. But so few in the Northern Kingdom have looked toward the truth that brings life."

Seer coughed and waited a minute until his breath returned.

"Do you know why?"

There was no response.

"It is because they never saw their rulers make the hard decision of putting away those statues. Two golden calves. Two pieces of wood covered with metal.

"How many lives they have cost.

"How many lives they will cost.

"What a waste of a kingdom."

"We have wanted to do the right things. I have. My father and grand-father did. Others who have sat on the throne wanted to do the right things. But there are realities to ruling this kingdom that the truth-tellers have never understood."

"Realities. We knew your realities. But there were much greater realities. . . . Open my window, that I might feel the wind," said the dying man to his servant. Then turning to the king he said, "Get a bow. Get a quiver of arrows."

The king went outside to his guard and was given a bow and quiver. The king strung it and returned to his friend's chamber. While he was gone the servant of Seer had helped him to a sitting position. A gleam still showed in the old man's eye as the young king returned to the room.

"Grip the bow tightly," said Seer. As the king held his bow, Seer placed his wrinkled hands on the king's hands and pointed the bow out the window. "Look in the direction of the Winding River and beyond to the City of Caravans. Take an arrow from your quiver and shoot toward the land beyond the river."

No king likes to do things that might look silly or foolish to those around. This king wanted to humor the dying truth-teller, but he quickly looked out the window to see if anyone might see him firing arrows at nothing. No one was about, so he pulled back the string and let the arrow fly fast and straight through the window.

"You speak of realities. Here is the reality: Truth-Holder is the victory, not Shining One or two gold statues," said Seer. "Because you came to me and listened to my words and followed my command, the one above all will give you the victory over the enemy that holds the land across the river."

Strong King looked toward the Mountains of the Dawn and smiled at the dream of regaining the lands that had been taken from his kingdom.

"Now, my son, grab a fistful of arrows from the quiver," said Seer, "and strike them upon the floor as many times as you wish."

The king grabbed a fistful of arrows and struck the floor. A guard heard the noise and looked through the opening. Again the king felt foolish. "It is all right," he said.

He struck the floor once more, trying to make less noise, and then he struck the floor a third time.

"Why have you stopped?" asked the old man with the little strength he had left.

Strong King had no answer.

"Here is another reality. You kings have feared to let your people worship in the sanctuary of Truth-Holder because it might not be easy. Truth-Holder wishes all your heart, not just a portion. So now Truth-Holder will give you a victory for every time you struck the ground. He would have made you stronger, if you had struck the ground more times."

"I struck it three times," said the king.

"And so you will have three victories over the army of the City of Caravans. You will just get by against your enemies, but soon this kingdom will be swept away. The northern kings have tried to rule with justice. But justice without truth must fail. Will you never learn that lesson?"

Seer motioned for his servant to help him lie down again. The king left the house and returned to his palace downcast, for the wisdom he would soon lose and for the truth he knew he had been told. But then again, he also had been promised great victories. Surely things were not so bad as the old truth-teller had said.

The next day he heard the news.

After he had left the house, Seer had closed his eyes and watched a golden chariot drawn by flaming stallions sweep down from the sky.

Listener waved.

Seer smiled.

And they rode off beyond the sky.

The Northern Kingdom mourned for the man who raised children from the dead and healed a foreign commander of a horrible disease and saved the capital from destruction. Here was a man of vision who could see the hand of Truth-Holder when most saw only the hand of fear. Seer's body was washed and wrapped and placed in its tomb on the day of his death. That was always the way of the People of the Promise. But people came from far away to mourn his passing. People came from the shores of the Great Sea and from the plains beyond the Winding River. People of the Southern Kingdom had also been touched by this great man, and some came many miles to weep at his tomb. For a brief moment grief united North and South once again. They became one as in the days of Shepherd and the days of Wise King.

The moment quickly passed, and no one really noticed what it meant.

Strong King went back to his army, and in the spring he led his men to war. Three times he met the king of the City of Caravans and three times he was victorious. In battle he won all the lands his father and grandfather had lost. The North was again a great kingdom and their enemies shuddered.

Yet the king of the South did not shudder, for he had also had his victories and felt himself a great king. He called the Northern King to battle.

Strong king gathered his army and marched into the land of the Southern Kingdom. There was a mighty clash, but the North was greater. It was then that the Northern Army returned from the Southern Kingdom bearing the Southern King in chains. They also attacked the great City of Palms.

They broke through the city walls
and ransacked the capital
and raided the sanctuary.

Strong King took little pleasure in this great victory, but he kept the Southern King a prisoner. "When I die," he told his oldest son, "send the Southern King back to his kingdom."

Strong King's sleep was restless and filled with accusing dreams.

"Why do you still cling to the golden calves?" demanded Seer. "Why did you raid the sanctuary of Truth-Holder? Why do you still hold the descendant of Shepherd King in your prison?"

Even in his dream, Strong King stood in guilty silence before the truth-teller.

Seer's eyes blazed. "How dare you treat Truth-Holder with such disrespect?"

Strong King backed up in fear and turned his face from the dead man.

"You have seen victory, but you have not followed the ways of the one beyond the sky. I showed you the hand of Truth-Holder, but you refused to see."

"What shall I do?" begged the king.

"It is too late," said Seer. "Tonight you shall leave the Blue Planet."

"But I am not ready," cried the king. "I will make everything right. I will release the Southern King and sacrifice a thousand spotless, newborn lambs and destroy the golden calves."

"The future holds much sorrow," said Seer. "Your grandchildren shall fall and your kingdom shall fall and in time the land of Shepherd King shall fall. The age of kingdoms shall soon pass away. The age of sorrows will begin."

"Is there no hope?"

"There is always hope," said the dream.

Strong King awoke. He was weak and fainthearted and beads of sweat rolled down his brow.

"Get my son," he told his servants. "I must speak to my son."

The young man rushed to his father's side as spasms of pain pressed against the king's chest. The father gripped his son's hand.

"It is time," said Seer.

"My son. . ." The king forced the words and gasped for breath.

"Release. . .release the Southern King," he pushed the words out.

Seer took his hand and the king wept.

"If your son follows your words, his reign will be stronger than was yours," said Seer. "He shall be known as the Prosperous King, but after him will come the sorrows."

"How much sorrow?"

"More than either kingdom could ever imagine."

"But there is hope."

"Yes," said Seer as he looked into the king's eyes. "Out of sorrow the one who is infinite and eternal and all-powerful shall plant seeds of hope and promise that will change the destiny of the Blue Planet."

The two men looked back on the capital city and watched as the son released the Southern King. They watched the son of the Southern King sacrifice a thousand spotless, newborn lambs. They watched a beautiful rainbow arch across the City of Palms.

"How majestic," said the Northern King.

"More than majesty. Much more than majesty," said Seer.

"I never understood," admitted the king.

"So many do not understand, but the truth is painted on the sky for all to see.

'He is always close and he will always care.' "

EPILOGUE

The storyteller stared at the sky for the longest time. People in the circle looked up, wondering if he watched the thin crescent moon or some far-off star.

"It's such a wonderful rainbow," the man with a hundred wrinkles said softly. "Its arch fills the sky."

"You must have sharp eyes, old friend, if you see rainbows when the sun isn't shining," said one shepherd with a laugh.

". . .And when there hasn't been rain for weeks," added another.

"Come here, little one," the storyteller called to his granddaughter. He lifted her up and pointed in an arc across the night sky.

"You see the rainbow, don't you? Its arch begins down there and swings all the way over there."

"Yes, grandfather, it is filled with all the colors."

"But how is it you see a rainbow, when no one else can?" he asked.

"I see it with my heart."

"That is a good answer. Sometimes one sees more clearly with one's heart than with one's eyes."

The old man turned to all his listeners.

"We have shared this fire together for thirty-one starry nights, a month of stories about the kingdom of our fathers, how it was put together and how it broke apart.

"I have told stories of King-Maker

"and stories of Hope-Giver

"and stories of Truth-Holder."

"But most of all I have told you about promises kept by the one beyond the sky, even through the darkest nights. Sometimes you can't see the promises, but those who look with pure hearts can always see the rainbow."

The girl looked from the night sky into the face of the storyteller.

"Grandfather, what if there were no rainbows?"

"For those who walk with the one who holds all those stars in his hands, there are always rainbows."

BEHIND THE STORIES. . .

Bible texts from 1 and 2 Samuel, 1 and 2 Kings, and 1 and 2 Chronicles inspired these stories. The corresponding Bible passages are:

The Secret Prince	1 Samuel 9–10:16
The First King	1 Samuel 10:17–13:18
The Last Chance	1 Samuel 15
The Shepherd Boy	1 Samuel 16
The Friendship	1 Samuel 17–20
The Fugitive	1 Samuel 22–25; Psalms 54, 57
The Woman of Darkness	1 Samuel 28; 31
The Shepherd King	2 Samuel 1–6
The Beguiling Beauty	2 Samuel 11–12; Psalm 51
The Rebel	2 Samuel 13–15; 17–18
The Numbering	2 Samuel 19–20; 24; 1 Chronicles 21
The Wise King	1 Kings 1–4; 1 Chronicles 22; 28–29
The Builder and the House	1 Kings 5–9
The Wise Fool	1 Kings 7; 10–11; Ecclesiastes
The Divided People	1 Kings 12:1–24; 2 Chronicles 10–11
The Warrior King	1 Kings 15:1–8; 2 Chronicles 12–13
The Good King	1 Kings 15:9–24; 2 Chronicles 14–16
The Sailor King	1 Kings 22:41–50; 2 Chronicles 17–20
The Wicked Queen	2 Chronicles 21
The Boy King	2 Kings 9:17–28; 11–12; 2 Chronicles 22–24:17
The Mighty Thistle	2 Kings 14:1–22; 2 Chronicles 25; Joel
The Dynasty of the Calf	1 Kings 12–13
The Dynasty of the Night	1 Kings 14–16:20
The Dynasty of the Castle	1 Kings 16:23–24; 20; 22
The Listener	1 Kings 17:1–18:18
The Contest	1 Kings 18:19–19:21
The Two Sons	2 Kings 1–3; 9:14–37
The Seer's Power	2 Kings 4–5
The Seer's Vision	2 Kings 6:8–8:15
The Dynasty of the Sword	2 Kings 9–10; 13:1–9
The Sad Farewells	2 Kings 13:10–25; 14:11–16